ChangelingPress.com

Sword/Viper Duet

Marteeka Karland

Sword/Viper Duet
Marteeka Karland

ISBN: 9798578034831

Publisher:
Changeling Press LLC
315 N. Centre St.
Martinsburg, WV 25404
ChangelingPress.com

Printed in the U.S.A.

Editor: Katriena Knights
Cover Artist: Marteeka Karland

The individual stories in this anthology have been previously released in E-Book format.

Table of Contents

Sword (Bones MC 3)

Marteeka Karland

Magenta: The day my mom took up with Black Reign was the worst day of my life. She became ol' lady for their president. I became another whore for the club to push around. I fought them at every turn because death was preferable to living this life. Beaten, downtrodden, I was about to be given to yet another man. The scariest man I'd ever seen. He was intent on having me on his own turf, and I wasn't sure I would survive.

Sword: The second I saw the slight young thing being beaten by that ogre of a man, something inside me I'd thought leashed broke free. A demon better left in check reared his head, and I knew she would be mine no matter what. I got her, but she came with bigger problems than I was prepared to deal with. Not that it mattered. I'm Bones MC. We don't give up, and we protect our own. Even against The Devil himself...

Chapter One

"This is a bad, fucked-up place if ever I saw one." Sword glanced at Torpedo, his brother in the Bones MC. They'd made the typically thirteen-hour trip to Lake Worth, Florida in just under twelve hours, riding non-stop as fast as they dared. Cain had sent a group of them to contact a club known as Black Reign. If their information could be believed, Black Reign was moving pills up the "Oxy Highway" from Florida to Kentucky. Cain couldn't care less what they sold or how they sold it, but he would not tolerate another club moving shit through their territory without the OK from Bones. Now, he lay on his belly watching the dingy brown clubhouse in the middle of a seaside urban sprawl.

"Yeah," Torpedo, their vice president, agreed. He had squatted down just behind Sword but still low to the ground. "I got a real bad feelin' about this."

Sword glanced at the other four men with him. Viper, situated in a similar position next to Torpedo, looked coiled with tension, ready to strike at the slightest provocation. Didn't mean anything, though. The man always looked that way. Trucker was impassive as ever, farther behind them and slightly to the left so he was hidden in the foliage but still able to see their target. He polished a huge wrench with a black rag as if he planned on working on one of their vehicles. The man always carried a gun, but Sword had never seen him use it outside their work with ExFil, a paramilitary mercenary company for hire to anyone wishing extra protection in the most violent areas of the world. He had seen Trucker open a can of whoop-ass more than once with that exact same wrench.

Arkham and Torpedo each checked various weapons on their person, readying for what was to come.

Torpedo was the vice president of the club and would do the talking. Cain had originally intended on coming himself, but Torpedo, Sword, and Bohannon had all three protested vehemently. Cain, ever the ultra-alpha, had gone nose to nose with the trio, and they might have come to blows except for one minor incident.

Angel, Cain's woman, had put a restraining arm on her man and pulled him away from his brothers. Though Cain routinely gave the woman anything and everything she wanted, he'd looked at her, a warning in his eyes for her not to go against him in front of his brothers.

"I know you need to do this, Cain," she'd said. At the time Sword thought she was ignoring Cain's warning. Instead, she'd had a very good reason. "But I need you more than the club needs you to go to Florida and confront these men." She'd said it softly, and there had been a sheen of tears in her eyes. Sword knew it was an intensely personal moment, but she'd brought it up in front of them. Now, they'd know what the problem was, and they'd all crush it for her.

Cain had known it, too. Any problem his woman had from the outside world, the club would know about it. They'd all band together and make it right, no matter the cost. "I can't let you tell me in private, Angel. Not now that you've brought it up in front of the club during club business. You shouldn't even be here." The president had been angry she'd snuck in. They could all tell from the look on her face, though, she had a good reason.

"Cain, I'm pregnant." There had been instant silence in the room. Cain had sucked in a short inhalation of air before grasping her by the shoulders. "Don't be mad because you think I was holding something back from you. I just found out today."

"Woman, you'd better start talking."

It turned out that Angel had gone to the doctor because she'd been weak and very sick over the last few weeks. Nothing abnormal for a pregnancy there. However, she'd hidden most of the sickness from everyone, and she'd reached a point where she was very dehydrated and, once her doctor figured out she was pregnant, he'd wanted her to be admitted for IV fluids and medication for nausea. She'd initially refused, not wanting to alarm Cain, but the oral meds the doctor had given Angel weren't working. She was unable to keep anything down and was afraid she'd harm the baby if she didn't go to the hospital like her doctor recommended. She was terrified of losing the baby and needed Cain at her side.

Bohannon, the club's main enforcer, had jumped all over that shit. "You can't leave her, Cain. You're not the kind of man to leave his woman to deal with this alone."

Cain had given the big man a withering look, but had readily agreed. He'd pulled Angel into his arms while the woman finally gave in to what had to be a horrible bout of nerves. She'd clung to Cain and silently sobbed into his shirt. They couldn't hear her, but the shaking of her slight body gave her away.

Naturally, Bohannon, as the main enforcer for Bones, had thought he'd go. If they were going to warn an MC out of their territory, they needed all the muscle they could get.

"You know that shit ain't happening." Torpedo had stood from his seat at the table where they'd gathered to hash out what to do in this situation. It was something they always did. Whether it was Bones or in preparing for a mission with ExFil, they talked through the problem and built a plan of attack together with Cain having the last say. "As vice president, I have to be there, especially since Cain has more pressing problems." He looked at Angel then, his eyes softening for the first time. "You make him take care of you and the little man who'll be the newest member of Bones," he'd said, serenity in his gaze and his voice. "With Cain focused on Angel, the club will need you here, Bohannon. You're third in the chain of command. Sword will come with me as enforcer. Trucker, as always, will provide the chase vehicle with the weapons. Viper and Arkham will be the muscle. Data can keep track of us and run communications from his command center here. If anything goes wrong, you can send whoever you see fit after us."

"It's thirteen fuckin' hours away, Torpedo! Any help I could bring would be hopelessly too late."

"Then we'll just have to make sure we don't need you. Besides, Salvation's Bane is less than half an hour away in Palm Beach. Thorn can send any help we need."

Luna, Bohannon's woman, curled her small hands around the enforcer's biceps. "They'll be fine, Bohannon. Let them do their jobs."

"Does every woman in this fuckin' place think she can take over the fuckin' show?" Bohannon grumbled, but his large hand enveloped his woman's smaller one in a loving gesture even as he groused.

"Only when the testosterone overflows. It reduces you to cavemen, and we can't have that."

Everyone chuckled, and the tension level dropped. Sword had never seen a club where the patched members let women in on meetings, but the women of Bones didn't seem to care for conventionality. They simply slipped in when they knew they were needed and directed the flow of churning water in the direction it flowed best. None of them had been with their men long, but Sword could already see the positive impact they were having. Simply keeping a group of alpha males like this one focused on the problem at hand without unnecessarily risking themselves wasn't an easy job, yet these two small women handled it like pros.

Now, as he lay on his belly watching the abandoned warehouse that served as clubhouse for Black Reign, Sword got the sickening feeling his team was undermanned. If they continued with the meeting as planned, they'd be walking into more muscle than they were prepared for.

"You gonna call in reinforcements?" Trucker's question was soft and nonchalant, as if the man could care less. It was a simple enough question. The fact Trucker asked it, however, showed he was thinking along the same line Sword was. Which meant that...

"Yeah. I think I am."

"Get Data to give the heads up to Thorn. He'll get Salvation's Bane ready in case we need them."

"Already on that, bro." He held up his cell phone. "All you gotta do is say the word. Thorn is less than five minutes away parked and waiting. Apparently, Bohannon jumped the gun and had them on stand-by over an hour ago. Surely to hell and God above we can last five minutes."

"Be embarrassing otherwise," Arkham chimed in. Though Sword was looking at the clubhouse through field glasses, Arkham and Viper were tracking the place with sniper rifles.

"Not sure I've ever met anyone as bloodthirsty as you and Viper." Torpedo was only half joking.

"We got movement." Sword stiffened as he watched as a big, burly man dragged in a woman by her hair. She screamed, clutching her hair to relieve the tension the big man had put on her scalp. The woman tried to back off, planting her feet, but the concrete was slick and unforgiving. She ended up on the ground, the man still dragging her by an abundance of hair. Two more women followed on their own. The latter chatted with each other, ignoring the drama in front of them. When the women passed the struggling couple, disappearing into the clubhouse, the hulking man pulled the woman to her feet and backhanded her across the face so hard she crumpled at his feet.

Sword's entire being shrieked in outrage. He couldn't see her face, but her legs and arms were firm and sleek with fine muscle, a testament of her youth. He thought she was an adult, but probably quite young. Protective instincts rose in him like never before, and it was all he could do to keep himself from charging to her rescue.

"Easy there, brother," Torpedo said, laying a restraining hand on his shoulder. "You know that girl?"

Had he said something out loud? "No."

"You're growling and tense like you intend to do some damage."

"You telling me you enjoy seeing young women beaten like that? Because I won't believe you."

"Not saying I do," Torpedo assured, his voice calming when everything inside Sword wanted to beat that motherfucker to a bloody pulp. "But we have to be careful here. This isn't our territory."

"I can't let an abused woman stay here if she doesn't want to, Torpedo. Neither can you."

"No. But we'll do it discreetly. Above all, we have to protect Bones and each other."

Sword ground his teeth. What good was having all these skills, not to mention selling his soul on the battlefield, if he couldn't protect the weak right in front of him?

Instead of replying to the vice president, Sword continued to look through the field glasses. When the girl got to her feet, he could see that, though she was short compared to the man, she was indeed an adult. Though, like he'd first thought, not by much.

Her hair was pale blond, nearly platinum, and hung past her hips in gentle waves where it wasn't tangled from the brute's handling of her. Creamy skin was flushed and bruising from the abuse she was currently sustaining. She bared white teeth at her attacker only to gain another backhanded hit that sent her spinning to the ground once more. He thought she was strikingly beautiful, but it was hard to say as blood splattered across her face. One cheek and her lip had begun to swell from the beating. She spat blood but got back up, yelling an angry epitaph at the man. He seemed unimpressed, grabbing her upper arm and yanking her inside. Sword's gut churned. He'd soon see her close up, if she was one of the club girls. Then he'd be better able to assess her injuries. If not, he'd figure out a way to get the president of Black Reign to bring her to him.

"Are we really goin' in there?" Viper asked the question in an almost bored tone. "Because, if we are, I gotta warn ya I doubt we'll make it back out without fightin' someone."

"Understood," Torpedo answered. "We've got another two hours before they're expectin' us. I suggest we rest in shifts. Sword, you, Arkham, and Trucker take an hour. Viper and I will go next."

Sword wasn't stupid. He knew Torpedo was doing this to distract him. Right now, he was fine with it. He was tired as a motherfucker. After a nap, he'd ready his gear and find his center. If he went into this meeting looking for a fight, there was no doubt he'd find one. While their brothers in Salvation's Bane MC knew the Florida Everglades well enough to dispose of a body, Bones didn't. Leaving bodies wasn't out of the question, but it was something none of them wanted to leave for their sister club to clean up.

For now, Sword would rest and try to put the girl out of his mind. Once he woke, he'd see more clearly what he needed to do.

Chapter Two

The order for girls had come down from Crow, president of Black Reign MC. Apparently, they were meeting with a club from Kentucky. Crow and Handlebar called them "dumb hicks who didn't know their ass from a hole in the ground," so Magenta had no reason to think this club was any different from the one she was currently with. Unwillingly though it might be.

Her mother had recently become ol' lady to Crow, though the man still had his share of women in the club. Her mother didn't seem to mind since she got whatever she wanted as long as she kept her nose out of club business. She wasn't after money. She had that already. Ginger wanted the power that came with being the ol' lady of an MC president. Especially one like Black Reign. Every woman in the area deferred to her, from the city council to the local PTA. Black Reign wasn't spoken of openly, but more than one person had found themselves doing things like cleaning up vandalism to their properties all the way to planning the funeral of a loved one, though that was rare. Ginger loved having that kind of power. And Black Reign wielded power without mercy.

Ginger thought her place in the club was solidified, but Magenta knew better. Ginger came from a family of wealth. Once he'd siphoned off everything he could, Crow would discard her, and Ginger would be either reduced to a mama or club lay, or banished from the club altogether. Being a mama would put Ginger in the position of being able to be claimed as an ol' lady but reduce her to prostitution. She'd have to earn her way in the club. Bring in her share of money. Being a lay for the club would reduce her even further.

Any member of the club could take her at will to satisfy any sexual urges they had at the time. That would be her contribution. While most clubs, including Black Reign, had casual hook-ups with the women in their ranks, in Black Reign they designated a few women specifically for sex with its members. No matter what they were doing at the time, if a man wanted to fuck, the woman he wanted had to stop what she was doing -- or not in some cases -- and the guy would do what he wanted. Magenta thought Ginger would end up as one of that number. Crow was paranoid enough to want to keep a close eye on Ginger once he was done with her, and sadistic enough to want to see Ginger brought to her knees. The man would enjoy watching his former woman being fucked by every patched member and prospect.

On the other hand, Magenta knew she herself was well and truly screwed no matter the outcome for Ginger. Crow would never let her go. Unless she was mistaken, he was just biding his time until he made a move on her. If he did, she'd resist in the most violent way she could. Which meant she would be beaten. If she was lucky, beaten to death. If not... well. They could keep her against her will until they tired of her. And she knew they'd all have a go at her. Death would definitely be preferable to her.

Handlebar had done a number on her face when he'd dragged her to the clubhouse. Her knees and legs were scraped and bruised too, so she had to wear jeans to cover up the mess. She had a leather vest she'd been instructed to wear because it was tight over her breasts and pushed the small mounds together enough to produce cleavage. Unfortunately, that also left her arms bare, the bruising over her fair skin visible where Handlebar had gripped her too tightly. Layers of makeup covered the worst of the bruising to her face, but, even after the ice packs and anti-inflammatories, there was nothing she could do about the swelling. Her long, thick, blond hair hung loosely in spirals down her back past her buttocks. Other than her hair, she definitely wasn't looking her best. Which was fine with her. Maybe she'd be spared this humiliation and could just go to sleep.

When she entered the common room of the clubhouse, a sectioned-off area where all the parties took place, she found five grim-faced men she didn't recognize entering from the front. All of them were scary as hell, and she had to force herself not to flinch. None of them looked as if he'd ever smiled in his life. There was a hard, deadly aura surrounding the lot of them. Cold, all-seeing eyes quartered every part of the room and assessed every person -- man or woman -- around them. It was hard not to stare, but she cast her eyes down and stood with the other seven women in the line. Introductions were made as the women lined up before Crow presented them to the rival MC.

"Our best," Crow said, sweeping a hand in their direction. Most of the women in the line with her giggled, trying to look coquettish. "As a warm welcome to Bones MC, you may choose your company for the night. We'll talk business tomorrow." Code for, "Our women will try to bleed you for every stitch of information they can get before tomorrow."

Torpedo, the vice president of Bones, shook his head, but another man put a hand on his shoulder, leaning in close to whisper something. "I suppose some of us might want some company to wind down after the long ride down here." He waved a hand at the girls in the line. "Boys, take your pick."

The one they called Arkham immediately came forward and snagged three of the women. All three went willingly, giggling all the way, telling him how good they'd make him feel. Arkham didn't say a word, just indicated for the women to take him to a room. The other members of Bones begged off except the one who'd stopped Torpedo from declining for all of them.

"Sword?" Torpedo raised a questioning eyebrow at him. Magenta shivered, lowering her gaze once more. When had she begun watching the men? While all five were striking in appearance, Arkham was by far the scariest with more than one scar decorating his face and strange, dual-colored eyes. This Sword wasn't so much scary as hard. She knew instinctively there would be no give to the man. Once he made a decision, he stuck to it. Men like that had a distinctive look in their eyes. This one more so than most.

"You." He stood in front of Magenta, but she steadfastly refused to look at him, going so far as to squeeze her eyes shut. And really, this was her worst nightmare. Every single time the club gave her to a visiting club she had to fight off her disgust to accommodate the men. None had ever been satisfied with her and she knew Handlebar would tolerate only so much more before he took her in hand himself. His lessons in pleasing a man were brutal at best. More than one woman hadn't survived his lessons and had become gator bait. He was called Handlebar for a reason. His favorite thing to do was to bend a woman over the handlebars of his bike and fuck her without mercy while both were astride the machine.

"Magenta," Handlebar said warningly. "Go with the man." She couldn't help shuddering and wrapping her arms around herself.

"Come with me," Sword said. "You'll suit my needs fine."

Handlebar sneered when she glanced his way. "After this, I'll be givin' you a lesson in obedience." Magenta had to bite her lip to keep from sobbing. Against her will, tears sprang from her eyes to cling to her lashes. She knew better than to blink lest they track down her face and ruin the makeup she'd so carefully applied to conceal her bruises.

Instead of taking her deeper into the Black Reign clubhouse, Sword steered her with a hand on her back toward the door. Until Handlebar stopped him.

"Where you think you're going with the bitch? She's club property."

"I don't fuck in another club's house," Sword said, meeting Handlebar's gaze with an icy one of his own. "Your president offered her. I'm taking her. She'll be returned when I'm done."

Handlebar stepped closer. Magenta knew it was supposed to be a threatening gesture, but Sword only met his advance with one of his own, putting himself between her and Handlebar. The two men stood nose to nose, except Sword had a good three inches on Handlebar.

Crow broke the tension with a chuckle. "Let it go, Handlebar. She's a whore. It's not like she's going anywhere. Besides, she'd never leave her mother here alone." Crow's smile turned to Magenta, and it was positively evil. She'd known this was coming. Apparently, Ginger's money was running out. Either that, or Crow was getting tired of her incessant whining.

Sword urged her forward with him. Magenta was surprised at how gentle his touch was. He didn't grab her upper arm like Handlebar always did. He nudged her, placing his hand on her shoulder, then the small of her back. He kept her going until they reached his bike. Once there, he handed her his helmet.

"Put this on."

"What about you?"

He didn't look at her, but straddled his bike and started it up. "I'm fine. Just get on so we can get the fuck out of here." He raised his voice over the engine, but spoke matter-of-factly.

She did as she was told. Not because she was afraid of him, but just the opposite. Other than decreeing he was taking her out of the clubhouse and would bring her back when he was finished with her, he hadn't asserted himself over her. Even that wasn't directed at her. He was careful of her bruises or, at the very least, didn't touch her too much for whatever reason. Sword wasn't a safe man by any means, but he didn't treat her as badly as the members of Black Reign did. At least, he hadn't yet.

Sword took her out into the night, the humid Florida breeze catching her long hair and whipping it back. Magenta wanted desperately to rip off the helmet and just let the wind overtake her. Because she was such a thorn in the side of the club, no one ever moved her on a bike. She was always put in one of the chase vehicles and lashed to something to ensure she didn't leap out of the truck and run.

She was possibly going to a bad place with a bad man, but Magenta couldn't work up the fear she should be feeling. Instead, when they stopped at a stoplight, she took off the helmet and lashed it to the back before the light turned green.

"What are you doin'? Put the fuckin' helmet back on."

"What does it matter? If you wreck and I die, I died with the sea air in my hair and the moon shining on my face, feeling free for the first time in my life. I never knew how thrilling riding a bike could be or how powerful it would make me feel!" There was no way to contain the breathless excitement in her voice.

"You've never ridden with one of your club members?"

"They always thought I'd bolt, so they never allowed me the privilege. Had I known how joyful this was, I might have behaved more like they wanted me to."

The light turned green, and Sword sighed. He sounded almost resigned. "Just hang on. I don't want you falling off the back." Then they sped off into the night.

Chapter Three

It was nearly two in the morning when Sword pulled into the overgrown abandoned lot where Trucker had parked the RV. He hadn't slept in nearly two days and was bone fucking tired. Still, he'd have gone another couple of rounds just to hear the musical laughter behind him.

What the fuck? From the moment he'd seen this girl being beaten on her way into the club he'd been fixated on her. And he knew Magenta was the same girl. It was all that hair that gave her away. So pale it was nearly white, there was just enough blond that when the sun shone on it, he knew it would shine as brightly as gold. He'd gotten her out of the clubhouse where he could better control the situation. Because there was no way he was giving her back. He'd pay whatever he had to, but he was keeping Magenta.

Once she'd confessed how much she loved riding, describing almost exactly how he felt about it, he knew he'd gladly ride until he dropped just to give her this pleasure. He nearly had. Sword was so exhausted he could barely keep his eyes open. Still, he'd have continued on but knew it wasn't safe. His reflexes weren't as sharp as they should be in this state.

When he shut off the bike and scrubbed a hand over his weary eyes, Trucker approached him. "Was getting worried. You good?"

"Yeah," he answered automatically. Was he good? Sword didn't know. Something inside him was shifting, and it was uncomfortable.

Trucker's gaze shifted to Magenta, who sat behind him, not moving. She was probably waiting for him to tell her what to do. "Who's the lovely lady you brought with you?" The man merely smiled at her, but

Sword felt Magenta stiffen behind him. Obviously, she thought Sword meant to share her with his brothers. Where before she'd laughed and squealed happily, now she was withdrawing. Sword didn't blame her.

"Magenta, this is Trucker. Magenta will be my guest for... a while." He'd almost said tonight, but knew that wasn't true. He wasn't giving her back to Black Reign without a fight. Too late, Sword recognized his mistake, one he wouldn't have made if he'd been on his game instead of nearly dead on his feet. Instead of deferring to his brother by introducing Magenta to Trucker, he'd introduced Trucker to Magenta, making it seem too much like they were a couple. It was only out of habit Sword hadn't offered Trucker's role in their club to an outsider. It might not seem like much to Magenta, but Trucker would recognize Sword was too damned close to the situation. The only thing worse would have been if he'd actually claimed the young woman as his own. Fuck. Who was he kidding? Sword knew it was only a matter of fucking time before he did.

"I see." Sword wanted to wipe the grin off Trucker's face. The man went on every run, every mission. He was their mechanical backup. Anything that went wrong with any of the bikes or guns or any of the numerous equipment and tools they needed, he could fix or replace on a moment's notice. He was a huge man, tall and heavily muscled. His frame had been shaped by working with heavy equipment since his teenage years. Everyone often forgot he was highly intelligent and perceptive. Trucker knew something was up, and it was well below Sword's brain. "Well, don't hurt yourself. Should I prepare for a quick getaway?"

Sword didn't answer. Instead, he tried to give Trucker his most intimidating stare, which the man only chuckled at. He could almost hear Trucker saying, "Well, ain't you cute?"

Taking care not to grab Magenta's bruised upper arms, Sword guided her to the RV where they all were staying. Inside, he found Torpedo and Viper sitting lazily at the eating table. Both men met his gaze with an annoyed one.

"We were giving you fifteen more minutes, then we were coming after you." Torpedo wasn't happy in the least. "If you hadn't sent a text every hour we'd have been on you long before now."

"And one word, Sword? Really? Not a location or anything?"

"None of your Goddamned business," Sword groused. "It's not like Data doesn't have a leash shoved up all our asses."

"True that," Viper agreed. "But we're in another club's territory. Kind of expected you to check in."

"I'm fully aware of that," Sword snapped. "Which is why I sent texts at all. I've been busy." Magenta was retreating further and further into herself. He could all but see the detachment happening, and it pained him like a fist to the gut. "In case you hadn't noticed, I have a guest."

"Ma'am," Viper said, dipping his head in acknowledgement. "Next time your man there decides to take you on a foray, remind him to check in with his parents, will you?"

That was it. Sword was about to go medieval on Viper. He would have, too, except that Magenta let out an unexpected giggle. The sound was like soft, tinkling bells, and just as addictive as her joyful laughter as they'd ridden down the highway through the night.

He'd opened his mouth to tell Viper to shut the fuck up, but instead sighed. That one split second where he'd registered Magenta's amusement was enough to clue Viper in to how the girl had gotten under his skin. Just as quickly as it had started, her giggles ceased, leaving a bleak, dismal void in their wake.

Viper grinned at Magenta, which made Sword want to pummel him all the more. "You take care of our enforcer, girl. He's a handful, but I bet you can handle him."

Magenta ducked her head, not acknowledging Viper at all. It reminded Sword of how she'd stood in that line of girls Bones was supposed to pick from. She'd obviously been terrified then. Gone was the carefree laughter, the freedom she'd admitted to feeling earlier. This woman was beaten down, obviously terrified of the life she was in and those around it.

Sword circled her thin shoulders with his big arm. He dwarfed her in size. Had to have several years on her in age, too. Hell, no wonder she was terrified. That alone would be enough. Yet, there was more. Much more if he was correct. The bruises on her face and arms told that story quite clearly.

"Come on, Magenta." He guided her to the back and his bunk. There were six bunk beds in the middle of the RV and one master bedroom in the back they'd converted into a storage room. Trucker had every piece of equipment he needed in that room organized exactly the way he wanted it. No one touched his shit. The bunk Sword had taken for himself on this trip was at the back across from the bathroom. He paused long enough at his bunk to snag a clean T-shirt and a pair of sweats from his duffel. They would swallow her whole, but she'd be comfortable. And he could examine her to see what damage that fucking bastard, Handlebar, had done to her.

He opened the door to the bathroom and handed her the clothes. "Need you to change. I'll do this as easy as I can and respect your privacy, but I need to see where you're hurt so I know if I need to get you medical attention."

She blinked at him. "I -- you want me to change in front of you?"

"I do."

Magenta nodded, a resigned look on her face. Obediently, she unbuttoned her vest. A lacy black bra encased her small breasts, nearly bringing Sword to his knees. Instead of giving in to the need to touch her, to arouse her into accepting him, he gently moved his hands over the bruises on her torso. Red bruises in the first stages of turning purple covered her belly, chest, and back. A nasty one curved around her back to the underside of her breast. Sword noted every time she winced, where she hurt the worst.

"Don't move," he said, turning back to his bunk and retrieving a jar of arnica cream. He returned, opening the jar and setting the lid on the vanity. "This is for inflammation. It should help dull the pain as well. I'll get you an ice pack and some Tylenol before we go to bed." He paused until she finally looked up and met his gaze. "Do you mind if I put this on you, Magenta? I don't want to touch you unless you're OK with it."

The girl looked so startled, Sword's heart actually hurt. Did she truly expect him to take what he wanted whether or not she wanted him to? What was he thinking? Of course that was what she thought. She'd obviously been whored out before. The other girls seemed to be fine with what they were doing, but not Magenta. Finally, she nodded, ducking her head and letting her arms fall to her sides.

"Look at me, girl." At first, she didn't move. Just stood there with her gaze on the floor. "Magenta." Sword softened his voice, doing his best to beguile her. To coax her into doing what he needed instead of simply complying with an order.

Finally, she raised her gaze to meet his. What he saw there broke his heart. Tears glistened in her eyes but didn't spill. He could see she was scared and deeply humiliated.

"Honey, I ain't gonna hurt you," he said, raising his hands slightly so she could see them. "I just want to ease your pain."

"So you can cause more?" Her voice was a mere thread of sound, heartbreakingly tearful.

"Absolutely not. Magenta, if you'll give me your trust in this, I swear to you, no one will ever hurt you again. Not me. Not Handlebar. Not anyone in Black Reign."

"You can't promise that." She sighed, but shrugged. "Do what you feel is best."

Sword could see that was all he was going to get out of her. Bring as impersonal and gentle as he could, he smoothed the cream over each bruise. Any cuts or scrapes that broke the skin, he cleaned carefully with peroxide and antibiotic ointment.

Once he'd finished with her upper body, he had her put on the T-shirt while he got the first-aid kit from a side panel next to the bathroom. She removed her jeans without being told but left her panties on. Probably testing him. Sword said nothing, simply grunted as he knelt before her. She had bruising to both hips and striping over her lower back and thighs, as if someone had taken a whip or switch to her. The welts disappeared into her panties, and he knew her buttocks would be much the same. He suspected it had been a switch to make the marks on her because it took skill to wield a whip to make such thin welts. Skill he doubted that bastard Handlebar had, judging by the way he carried himself. Looks could be deceiving, but every man in Bones was adept at reading people from their body language. They had to when going on a mission with ExFil, Cain's paramilitary protection agency.

"I need you to lower your panties over your buttocks. Several of the welts and scratches go beneath them and need to be treated. Will you let me finish this?"

She nodded slightly before lowering her underwear just over her cheeks. No matter how hard he tried to make this impersonal, Sword winced every single time she did. Every single mark on her lovely body pained him like nothing else ever had. He smeared the antibiotic ointment over each break in the skin in a thin layer after cleaning the wounds with peroxide, trying his best to be gentle. Only two required a bandage. She made a small protest but settled with one look from him. The girl was definitely beaten down. The longer they stood there, more she trembled. When one tear overflowed, and she turned her head away immediately, Sword had had enough.

"Put the sweats on. They'll be way too big for you, but baggy will be good at this point. You need room to move and not hurt your legs any more than necessary."

She blinked up at him in confusion but did as he asked while Sword put away the first aid kit. "If you need to do your business after that long ride, do it. And don't think about tryin' to climb out the window either. Trucker is outside, and he sees and hears everything. You might make it outside, but you won't get far."

He hated that he was adding to her distress, but he couldn't have her running off. Not because she was afraid of them hurting her. Afterward, once he'd freed her completely from Black Reign, he'd give her the choice of a life with him or leaving club life altogether. At least, that was what he told himself.

Chapter Four

Magenta stood in the small but surprisingly clean, bathroom in the Bones RV. Sword had undressed her, had touched her body at will... and hadn't molested her? Had that really just happened? He'd been given the use of her body by Black Reign, and had every right within their community to take what was offered whether she wanted him to or not. Yet he hadn't. True, he'd forbidden her to leave, but she could understand that. Instead, he'd given her privacy and treated her with respect.

Offering him the same in hopes they could continue with the truce, she hurried her business, washed up, and exited the bathroom as quickly as she could. She found the men at the table deep in quiet conversation. They stopped talking and looked at her when she closed the door. Instantly, her heart pounded and her mouth went dry. Was this all a preamble to a gangbang? Had she truly been stupid enough to be lulled by Sword's tender touch?

"Get that look off your face, girl," Sword snarled at her, making her put a defensive hand to her throat and step back. "No one is going to hurt you."

"You growlin' at her like that ain't conducive to her believin' you, Sword," Torpedo said with a chuckle. "We're not the big bad wolves, Magenta."

She raised her chin a fraction, needing to face this head-on. If they were like Black Reign, there was every possibility they'd kill her for her insubordination. Not the best of options, but better than being gang-raped by such powerful-looking men. She wouldn't survive either encounter.

"Why should I believe you? You brought me with you to use at your leisure. You accepted me as a whore from another club whether I wanted to be here or not. Why should I think anything different?"

"Girl's got a point, Sword. What did you expect her to think? I mean, this was all your idea. Torpedo was gonna just leave, but you wanted a girl for the night."

"Shut your fuckin' mouth, Viper." Sword snapped the command, to which the other man chuckled. "I brought you with me to get you out of that place, Magenta. Not to hurt you. I also ain't takin' you back." He turned back to Viper. "She was the girl we saw that bastard Handlebar beatin' the shit out of as they dragged her inside the clubhouse. She's been beat more than once. She's got welts all over her."

Magenta was surprised Sword didn't describe it all in great detail, if for no other reason than to humiliate her. She was even more surprised when both Viper and Torpedo's attention snapped squarely to her.

"Was it all Handlebar or others?" Viper looked deadly. Like his namesake ready to strike.

"There is no member of Black Reign in charge who doesn't treat all the women badly. Some like it. Others tolerate it or figure out how to please the men without getting beaten. It's not always possible, but they try."

"They. Not you." Sword's gaze never strayed from her face. Much as Magenta wanted to look away, she couldn't. She'd started this. Apparently, these three men were going to make her finish it.

"No. Not me. It's why I'm always getting beaten."

"What did Handlebar mean when he said you and he needed to have a lesson in obedience?" Sword asked. "And I assume they have your mother prisoner, too."

"Handlebar will beat me again. He's done it so many times for the same reason, and I think he's getting fed up. Never a good thing. As to my mother, she's Crow's ol' lady. At least, she is until he gets tired of her. I suspect he's reached that point."

"Does she have any influence over Crow regarding you? Are you Crow's child?"

"No! Crow isn't my father, and I couldn't be happier about it!" She wrapped her arms around her middle. She was giving away too much, letting her mouth run away with her. Deep inside, she knew her willingness to give away information about herself and Black Reign stemmed from her high after the motorcycle ride earlier. And it truly was a high. Even now she was still coming down, feeling shaky and strung out. What's more, she resented it. Not because of anything Bones had done to her, but because Black Reign had restrained her. "I'm honestly not sure my mother knows or cares what Handlebar does. It doesn't affect her so why would she bother?"

"Crow indicated you'd come back to them because he had your mother. Why would he do that if you don't get along with her? Why would he believe you'd do anything other than cut and run if you got the chance?"

"I don't have it in me to leave her. At least, not without giving her the option of going with me. If I do, she'll tell Crow. Crow will tell Handlebar, and they'll have me before I ever make it to the door. Unless Crow sets her aside, though, I know Ginger won't leave. She believes her position with Crow is permanent, but I'm pretty sure Crow is just bleeding her for everything her parents gave her."

"Your grandparents are dead, then?"

"Yeah. She was their only child, and they left her everything, including a substantial insurance policy."

"What about you?" This question came from Torpedo. All three men were focused intently on her, but Torpedo was the worst. Sword's gaze shifted from her to the other two men, but he remained silent. "Did they leave you anything?"

"No. But I don't think Crow believes that."

"He'll definitely want her back," Sword said. "He'll want to make sure she doesn't have anything out there he can take." He glanced at Magenta again. "You think he'll try to move you into your mother's place?"

She shrugged. "Maybe. More likely he'll just demand I give him anything I have. He may claim me, but it won't be as an ol' lady."

The men looked at each other for long moments. Finally, Viper sighed. "I'll talk to Cain. Let him know the situation." He looked back at Magenta. There was resignation and amusement in his eyes. "Lord knows he's gonna kick your ass when we get back, Sword. Can't say it won't be worth a beatin', though. Might plead your case for you just to have a shot at beatin' the shit outta that fuck Handlebar my own damn self."

The three of them stood. "I'll go relieve Trucker," Viper said. "He's the only one of us who ain't had sleep. Well, except for Romeo over there. Maybe Arkham, but he don't count since he's balls deep in Black Reign women. We'll have a long day tomorrow. Get as much sleep as you can."

Sword stood and strode back to Magenta. He guided her to his bunk and urged her onto it. She protested slightly, but he merely looked at her until she meekly crawled onto the narrow mattress. It was about as wide as a twin-sized bed, and she was relieved that there was no way he could fit in there with her. Likely he was going to sleep on the top bunk…

Sword crawled into bed with her, turning her to her side and spooning against her. "This is all that's happenin' tonight, Magenta. Just relax and know that I'm watchin' over you. No one is gonna hurt you. Anyone tries, they answer to me."

She was quiet for a while, thinking about her situation. Magenta had so many questions she had no real idea where to start.

"Say what's on your mind, girl." Sword's rough, gravelly voice was soft in her ear. His breath made her shiver, and chills erupted over her arms and neck.

She cleared her throat, not sure how to start. "Did you ride me all over the place to disorient me? So I wouldn't know where I was if I tried to escape?"

Sword was silent for so long, Magenta thought he wouldn't answer before he finally sighed, his body relaxing around hers. "No. I did it because you seemed to love it so much. I guess I'm a sucker because once I realized you did, I had to give it to you. I only pulled in here because my eyes felt like someone had thrown sand in them. I hadn't had any sleep in forever. Otherwise, we'd probably still be out on the Goddamned highway until you called it a fuckin' night."

"What?" She whipped her head around to look at him the best she could in the dark. There was truth in his eyes. Magenta had long ago learned to read lies. Unless someone was extremely adept at it, she could tell when she was being played. Sword wasn't trying to deceive her. In fact, he looked uncomfortable as hell.

"You heard me," he groused. "Now, can we fuckin' get some sleep? I'm fuckin' tired."

For some reason, Magenta had the urge to push him. See how far she could go before he got angry with her. She must be out of her mind. "You asked what was on my mind. I was telling you."

"Fine. What else?"

"What are you going to do with me?"

"Nothin' until we take care of Black Reign."

"So, after that, then."

He gave an exasperated huff. Magenta could hear the weariness in that exhalation of breath even though she was sure he intended for her to only hear his annoyance. She was being a bitch for making him talk to her, but she wanted to know where she stood.

"I just want to get you to safety. Is that so hard to believe?" When she said nothing, Sword continued. "Now, let me ask you a question. When you said Handlebar would beat you, you implied he might do worse."

"So?"

"What's the 'worse' he'd do?"

Try as she might, even knowing he was going to ask this exact question, Magenta couldn't suppress the shudder that went through her body. "Handlebar isn't exactly known for his gentle handling of women. Especially when he fucks. He's called Handlebar for a reason." When he didn't say anything she continued. "He fucks women over the handlebars of his bike. I once saw him tie a woman's hands to the front wheel and her ankles to the pipes. He kept her there for days. Used her. It wasn't so much the sex for him as the violence he got off on. He loved knowing he was hurting that woman. He even rode around the compound with her tied to his bike, him with his dick inside her. Her legs and feet were badly burned. Sometimes I can still hear her screaming." Magenta had to stop and take a deep breath. Remembering the horror she'd witnessed was its own form of torture.

"Why did you watch?" Sword's arms snaked around her tightly, holding her to him in a protective embrace she hadn't expected to enjoy. For whatever reason, it made her feel safe. Probably because of his confession that he'd ridden half the night because he knew she was enjoying it. No one had ever done something like that for her. Especially at the expense of their own comfort.

"He always makes us watch. All the women. Well, except for Ginger. Her status as Crow's ol' lady keeps her from the worst of it, but she knows what goes on."

"She know he's got something like that planned for you?"

Magenta didn't know for sure Handlebar did. But she suspected he was just biding his time. Likely after they brought her back to the clubhouse, he'd make his move. "Probably. She's self-centered and doesn't care much about anyone else in the club as long as she gets what she wants, but there isn't much going on she doesn't know about. She might not acknowledge it, but she knows. No man they've ever given me to has ever been satisfied with me. I fight too much. Even the ones who want their girls to fight say they feel cheated. I guess I just fight harder than some of them. The only thing I have they can't take from me is my will. They may get what they want in the end, but I've never stopped fighting anytime it happens."

"It ends now, Magenta." Sword whispered in her ear. "You don't wanna go back, you don't go back. If you want us to give your mother an out, we will, but you're not goin' back."

"Am I to trade one prison for another? You keeping me against my will, too?"

"No. I'll see you safely back to Bones territory. Where you go from there is up to you. Doesn't mean you have to leave once we're home, though. You can become part of Bones until you're ready to make it on your own."

"Any pay I earn is mine. I'm not sharing with anybody." That sounded harsh, but she wasn't turning her earnings over to a club ever again. "I had my body used and abused more times than I want to think about after my mom got us mixed up with Black Reign. I took the punches, and they took the money. I leave there, it never happens again."

"Fine. Anything else?"

"Wow. No argument over that?"

"None. Mainly because you will never be whored out or sell yourself ever again. Not as long as you're with Bones. We ain't into that. There are plenty of things you can do to earn your keep and money to start a new life. Cain, our president, owns a paramilitary protection unit for hire. We make a decent living and so does the club. I'm sure he can find something for you to do in the office."

"You sound confident of that."

"There's always work. Maybe not glamorous work, but work. If you're willing, that is."

She thought about that for a while before responding. "I think that's fair. Assuming you're able to get me out of here. Word is Black Reign is out to destroy Bones. They're coming at you all nice right now, but they know you have their drug shipment and they want it back. You don't give it to them, they'll kill every last one of you and your families."

"We expected nothing less."

"I hope you got a plan because I guarantee you Crow does. He'll execute it brutally."

"None of us ever go anywhere without a plan." He didn't elaborate and Magenta didn't ask further.

Chapter Five

A soft, cool breeze fanned over Magenta's face. A soft heartbeat and the low hum of a fan were the only sounds around her. She was cocooned in warmth but couldn't figure out where she was. The familiar fear that swamped her upon waking didn't close around her. There was no feeling someone was watching her, ready to pounce. Of course, once she realized that, her pulse jumped and her mind warned her to be watchful and very afraid. The second her body tensed, the soothing cocoon tightened slightly. A deep, masculine grunt was the only other sound. That steady heartbeat didn't waver even a moment.

Sword.

She was in Sword's arms. In a ridiculously small bed. Fully clothed in his shirt and sweatpants. At some point, she'd sprawled out on top of him, her hair tangling them together like silk bindings. One of his big hands rubbed soothingly up and down her back in comfort. That hand seemed to span the entire width of her back as he moved it over her skin lazily.

Magenta remembered him sliding into the bed with her, wrapping her up in his arms as they'd talked. Their conversation spun through her mind like a carousel. Did she believe everything he'd told her? She wanted to. Though she knew better, Magenta decided she'd believe him until he misplaced her trust. Didn't mean she'd do it blindly, though. Maybe she should lay it all out for him.

"You're fine, girl," he murmured sleepily. "We got an hour before we need to get up."

"You know, if you're trying to make me give up information on Black Reign, I'm more than happy to do it without you making me empty promises. Just promise you won't make me go back, and I'll tell you everything I know. That's the only promise I want or need."

He sighed, as if disappointed. "I just want another hour," he grumbled. "Fine. Magenta, I promise I won't make you go back. Think I said that earlier. Now, go back to sleep. You can spill it all later."

"You're kind of a grumpy bear when you wake up, aren't you?"

Again, he grunted, but tightened his arms around her.

"What are you going to do? You left a man in the clubhouse so you can't just blaze."

With an exasperated grunt, Sword rolled them both, maneuvering so that he lay sprawled on top of her, his arms still wrapped around her. He nuzzled her neck, his lips grazing her skin in a soft caress. "Hush now. I need this last hour." He didn't stop moving his mouth over her neck.

"Stop," she whispered, even as she lifted her chin and tilted her head to give him better access. What was wrong with her? Was she going to let him take advantage of her? God, her body had suddenly come alive! Shivers coursed through her, and she realized that, for the first time in her life, she was welcoming a man's touch.

"Is that what you want?" Sword asked, even as he licked her flesh with one swipe of his flattened tongue. "You didn't push me away. Instead, if I'm not mistaken, your little nails are diggin' into my back like you're trying to hold me to you." He sounded drowsy. Sexy. Like he was her lover waking her for morning sex.

"I -- I don't know..."

"It's OK," he said between nips and scrapes of his teeth. "I'm not gonna take too big a bite out of you. At least not here or now." He let his lips wander from her neck to her collarbone and back, never venturing into forbidden territory but arousing her like she'd never been before. "When we go to confront Black Reign, you're staying here with Trucker."

"You'll need every man you have," she breathed out, scarcely able to form a coherent thought beyond the fact that she wanted to cradle his head and push him to her aching breasts. "Crow will annihilate you if you don't. In fact, call in help. He's trying to lull you into a false sense of security before he springs whatever trap he has ready."

"I promise you, the four men we're takin' into that clubhouse will be better equipped to deal with that entire club than Crow will be to deal with the four of us. But, you're right. We called in reinforcements last night. There will be some friends of ours coming to help. Should be here in a little over an hour." He shifted his weight off her just a little, just enough for her not to feel trapped. Then he laid his head on her chest and kissed the swell of her breast. "So I'd like to get my..." he raised his head to look back over his shoulder at the clock on the wall next to them, "fifty-four minutes."

"Yeah. So would me and Viper."

"If you guys need to get a room, you should have said something instead of staying out all fuckin' night ridin'."

"You two shut the fuck up. I'm determined to get my 'fifty-four minutes.'"

"Fifty-three now, bro. Shut up your own damned self."

Magenta didn't know what to think or say. Lying with Sword like this was too intimate for strangers, but, strangely, not uncomfortable. All kinds of things went through her mind. What if the others expected him to have sex with her right there? Did he expect that? If she gave in and embraced the sensations he kindled, would he humiliate her like Black Reign had? And what about Trucker? If everyone thought she'd given in to Sword, would they expect her to service them as well?

"Just relax," Sword whispered. "No one is gonna hurt you."

"You keep saying that."

"You need to hear it."

"Does me hearing it make it any truer than if you never said it?"

There was a long silence, and Magenta thought he'd dozed off. Then he lifted his face and kissed her throat, blazing a hot trail to her lips where he lingered a moment before pushing off her and getting to his feet. "I'll wake you before we leave," he whispered. "Get some more sleep. It will be a long ride home."

With that, he hopped up onto the bunk above her. Immediately, Magenta felt his rejection like a brutal punch. Realistically, she knew she couldn't have it both ways. She either wanted his touch or she didn't. She was scared and had voiced her reservations about how safe she was with him. He'd responded with the only option open to him.

It was better this way. Really. She'd take him up on his offer of a job and a place to get on her feet, then she'd get the hell out of Dodge. No fuss, no muss. And no awkward attachments.

Except there was one problem. Either she trusted him, or she didn't. If she didn't, then going back to his club with this group of men was stupidity embodied. If she did, they why was she making it so hard on him? Sure, he'd kissed her. He'd held her while she slept. He'd even calmed her fears when she'd first wakened. And she'd kicked him out of bed.

Fuck. This was getting her nowhere. She could go round and round in her head all fucking day and not be any closer to an answer. In the end, she had to trust her own judgment. While her mind was calling her all kinds of an idiot, her instinct was telling her to give the man a chance. He'd been good to her. God knows what would be happening to her right now if he hadn't taken her back with him. She was in the middle of his club. The only woman. And they weren't making her service them. Not even Sword. He'd calmly kissed her before taking a different bed. No harsh words. No abuse. Just calm acceptance. He hadn't even threatened to take her back to Handlebar and let him deal with her. In fact, he'd sworn he'd never take her back.

Confused as ever, Magenta turned to her side and closed her eyes. She had fifty minutes before they all got up. She'd rest until they stirred. Then she'd apologize to Sword. If nothing else, she needed to properly thank him for the ride when he was so tired. That was a miracle in itself. One she would remember for the rest of her life.

Chapter Six

Three motorcycles pulled up next to the RV. The three men were part of a sister club of Bones, Salvation's Bane, located in Palm Beach. Along with the four who'd planned on going into the Black Reign compound, they should be good to go.

"What's the op, Top?" They were addressed by the vice president, Havoc. He, Vicious and Carnage were not only part of Salvation's Bane, but employed by ExFil and men trusted by Bones.

"Got a club down here trying to run drugs through our territory without permission," Torpedo said to the other man. The two shook hands in greeting. "Wouldn't worry about them except they might take exception to us keeping one of their women who was being held against her will."

"You called us out here over a woman?" Havoc tried to look put out, but didn't quite pull it off. None of them would hesitate to help women and children if needed.

"Give me a break." Torpedo waved the other man off. "It was the four of us against an entire club. We're crazy. Not suicidal."

"You mean, four of Bones' elite Special Forces bikers can't take on one group of badass wannabes?" Havoc grinned. "You guys must be slipping."

They all chuckled together, slapping each other on the back in friendly greeting. "Anybody other than the one girl we gotta get away clean with?"

"Possibly her mother," Sword answered. "She needs to be given the opportunity to come away with Magenta."

"You don't sound hopeful."

"If I'm right, her mother's tied closely with the club. She's ol' lady to Crow, their president, and I think she's perfectly happy with the arrangement. Magenta says she's privy to everything goin' on. While she probably doesn't have much say, she could have prevented them from harmin' Magenta."

"What does she have to do with the drugs? Sounds like you called us here under false pretenses."

"Not at all." Torpedo shrugged. He had definitely made the problem of the drug running the focus of the request for aid, but it was far from the most pressing matter. "We confiscated the shipment they tried to exchange with another club. Normally, we wouldn't have interfered except they did it in the middle of our fuckin' territory. That kind of blatant disrespect can't be tolerated."

"But..." Havoc prompted with a wave of his hand.

"No buts about it. We confiscated their shit and destroyed it. They're pissed."

"Where does the girl fit in?"

"She's mine." Sword wanted no mistake about this. "They're not gettin' her back, and I refuse to get her out without even tryin' to get her mother to safety. Woman may not want to leave, and that's fine. But she's gonna have a chance."

"Fair enough. You should know that the Black Reign clubhouse is a very basic design. Easily penetrated. Not so easily defended."

"I could have told you that," Viper grumbled. "Completely bass-ackwards."

"Yes. But did you know you could get into their compound beneath the floor?"

"Maybe. If I'd been able to pour over the fuckin' blueprints like you've probably been doing since we called you."

"No, you wouldn't. It's not in the current blueprints. There's an old maze of underground tunnels abandoned because of flooding. They aren't in any official map or blueprint of the area. The building they bought was constructed with the remains of a Spanish villa of some sort. Didn't get the exact specs, but it was apparently originally built sometime in the mid-seventeen-hundreds. Not sure why the tunnels were built considering how close to the water table the place is, but they probably weren't used long."

"Then how do you know they're even still usable?"

"Because we looked at the site as a possible place for our setup a few years back. The tunnels were the very reason we wanted it. We abandoned it because of the defensive problems it presented, and it was in the middle of the city. Too close to prying eyes. Since Black Reign's into drug trafficking, it probably makes it easier for them to do business. From what we could find, they've fortified those tunnels like we'd planned on doing. Talked to a few of our local contacts. Found the men who worked on it. Sweet setup. They can take in shipments from the harbor without suspicion."

"So, they'll send all their firepower our way, leavin' the tunnels either abandoned or guarded with one or two men at most." Torpedo was nothing if not intelligent. This was strategy 101.

Havoc shrugged. "They're not what one would call the most thorough of planners. At least, not under Crow. If they could get a decent president in there, they might actually become a threat."

"So, we go in the front. Out the back," Torpedo said. "If all goes well, we won't need that back exit. We can just walk out no problems. I plan on trying to end this without a fight, but I don't anticipate that will happen. I need you guys to post up outside, ready in case things go sideways."

"Carnage and Vicious are our best snipers. They'll have eyes on you at all times. Since we looked at this place, we know where the best angles are."

"I'll leave it to you guys to do your thing, then. Let us know when you're in place, and we'll head that direction."

"Keep the dirty side down, brothers," Havoc said as he clasped hands with Torpedo, bringing him in for an affectionate slap on the back. "We've got your backs."

Trucker fitted everyone with a tiny earpiece. Their watches were already fitted with microphones to allow ease of communication. Everyone, including the snipers, had suppressers for their guns. They were as ready as they could be.

As the group from Salvation's Bane sped off, Sword and the others went back to the RV to ready their equipment. Before Sword and Magenta had gotten back from their ride, Trucker had placed a few cameras so he and Data could monitor everything going on outside the place. Arkham had done his job as well, planting several cameras inside the clubhouse. There was no audio, but it provided a measure of security for the upcoming confrontation and leaving the cameras in place would help keep tabs on a rival club for both Bones and Salvation's Bane. Sword had no idea how the man managed to wear out all three women he'd chosen, but a couple hours after Bones had left him, the first signals started coming in. By the time they'd returned to the RV to ready their equipment, every single room in the clubhouse was bugged.

Trucker and Data watched the displays together. Data from Kentucky while Trucker was ready to lend aid with the big guns if needed. If that happened, all hope of getting out of Florida unnoticed would be out the window. They'd ridden without their colors, only wearing them when visiting the Black Reign clubhouse. Tonight, none of them would have colors but Arkham, since he'd stayed behind. The second they were away, they'd stash their jackets until back in Bones territory.

Everything was ready. Sword's brothers were ready to ride, yet he stood inside the RV, looking down at one small woman. He'd told her he'd wake her before they left, but what was the point? She hadn't moved since he'd left her bed, hugging her pillow much like she'd hugged him to her. She probably hadn't slept easily for a long time, and he hated to disturb her. Instead, he knelt beside her bed and brushed a light kiss over her cheek.

Magenta's eyelashes fluttered and she whimpered a little, but didn't wake. "Rest easy, girl. I'll come back when we're done and get you the hell outta here."

"Sword?" She mumbled in her sleep, reaching out a hand. Sword took it immediately, brushing his lips over her fingers.

"Everything's good, baby. Go back to sleep."

"Don't get hurt," she said, her eyes still not opening. "Sorry I kicked you out of bed."

He couldn't help but chuckle. "No worries. I'll come back, and we'll ride home together on my bike.

You'll have all night to ride with the wind in your hair."

"Does that mean I'm riding bitch?" She smiled and opened her eyes slowly. The impact of those clear blue eyes hit Sword like a punch to the gut. She was so fucking beautiful it hurt. Like some kind of angel. Not fallen, but here to save his soul and bring him to heaven with her.

"No, baby. No one's ever gonna use the word bitch to describe you or anything about you. Even ridin' with me."

"Are you angry with me?"

"No. Never."

She reached out and laid her hand on the side of his face. It was all Sword could do not to close his eyes and lean into her touch.

"Maybe we could try it again after we get back to your club. I still want to go."

"We can do that. For now, just rest. Sleep as much as you can. It's a long ride back to Kentucky."

"Why are you so nice to me?"

"Because you need someone to be nice to you. And I'm such a nice man."

She giggled softly, the sound wrapping around his body like an erotic tether. What the fuck was he going to do with her? "I guess that's why they named you Sword. Because you're so nice."

"Now you're gettin' it." His smile came easily with her, when he wasn't a man to smile often. "When we get home, I'll introduce you to Angel and Luna. They're both new to our club as well. Angel is our president's ol' lady, and Luna is our enforcer Bohannon's. They'll help you adjust."

"You sound like I'll be staying a while."

"Well, you want a good chance to get on your feet. Right? You'll have to be there more than a few days. They're good people. They'll be nice to you."

"What about you?"

"I'll be nice to you, too." She opened her mouth to say more, but Sword cut her off with a light kiss to her mouth. A mere brushing of lips. "We'll discuss it later. Right now, I've got work to do. Try to sleep more if you can. If you can't, do not, under any circumstances, leave this RV unless Trucker tells you to. I'll be back as soon as I can."

She gripped his shirt in one tiny fist. "Don't leave me here alone, Sword. Right now, like it or not, you're my rock in this mess. I can't leave here without you."

"You won't, baby."

He brushed another kiss over her mouth then left. Sword had never really thought about leaving anyone behind before. It had always been just him and his brothers, most of whom were usually with him. This time felt... different. There was an ache in his chest that had never been there. A responsibility to make sure this woman was taken care of if he didn't come back. It was a decidedly uncomfortable feeling.

They got the signal from Havoc and his crew. Sword, like the other three members of his team, fitted their guns with silencers before holstering them. Straddling their bikes, readying to leave, each member went through their own pre-battle ritual. As he put on his helmet, Sword beckoned Trucker to him.

"If things go way south, I want you to promise me you'll get Magenta back to Kentucky. Don't let that bastard Crow get her back."

"She seems like a good girl. Intelligent. Certainly keeps you in line. I'll take care of her."

"Get her to Luna and Angel. They'll help her."

"You got it, brother. You guys get in. Get out. Rip it up. Anything else and you risk second-guessin' yourself. That's the quickest way to getting killed." Trucker smacked the side of Sword's helmet before walking away.

Rip it up. Be aggressive in everything. That's exactly what Sword planned on doing.

Torpedo gave the signal, and they all started their bikes. Black Reign was about to learn no one fucked with Bones.

Chapter Seven

As they entered the gate to the Black Reign property, Sword noticed a vast difference from their previous meeting. Now, guards were out in force, guns clearly visible. Not just handguns either. These men were heavily armed with AK-47s and other assault rifles. Judging by their stance and the way they held their weapons, most of the men had no idea what they were doing. Sword made note of every man who looked like he'd handled a weapon before and wasn't just mimicking the look of actors on TV. Those were the men he'd take out first.

The group of three rode into the compound without hesitation or any sign of fear. Crow, the president of Black Reign, met them just outside the clubhouse, flanked by three of his muscle. Of the three, Sword noted only one looked to have any experience. He focused on the surrounding area, looking for the men he couldn't see but knew were with Bones. He was younger than Crow and the other men by several years but was by far the most experienced.

Sword slid into place just behind Torpedo with Viper on Torpedo's other side. Once the bikes were shut down, both men took up defensive positions on either side of Torpedo, protecting him as much as they could by keeping eyes on the Black Reign men surrounding them so Torpedo could do their business with Crow.

Inside, members of Black Reign were scattered around the room, women draped over a few of them. A couple men checked weapons, making a show of loading and chambering a round. The place stank of pot and stale sex. There had obviously been a party after Bones left. Despite the appearance of raucous behavior and a rowdy party, the tension in the clubhouse was so thick, the hair stood up on the back of Sword's neck. Something was definitely off.

"I don't see my girl with you. Are you stealin' our women as well as our fuckin' drugs now?" Crow looked livid. More, he looked scared. Which was good. If he feared Bones, he respected them. But there was a little itch between Sword's shoulder blades. Something was off.

"The girl didn't want to return. We're under no obligation to help you hold someone against their will." As vice president, Torpedo spoke for the group.

"Bullshit! She's our property. You took her in good faith. You'll return her or none of you will leave this place alive."

"From the looks of things when we came in, you don't plan on us leavin' alive anyway. Besides, I doubt you're upset over one little female."

Crow's smile was evil. "Well, there's still the matter of the smack you stole. We're gonna to need it back."

"It's gone," Torpedo said without hesitation so there could be no mistake he meant what he said. "We destroyed it that very night."

"You mean you sold it. Or used it so your little hick club could get high. Party. Either way, you either give us our stuff, or you reimburse us." Crow sneered. "Or you don't leave this fuckin' place alive."

The clicks of safeties being switched off and rounds being chambered from every automatic and semi-automatic weapon in the room punctuated Crow's words. The Bones members didn't rise to the bait. They stood there, seemingly relaxed when every single one of them -- and the men listening outside -- were on high alert.

"You seem pretty confident you've got us."

"I am." Crow crossed his arms over his chest and nodded to the side where two men emerged with Arkham, hands behind his back. The big man looked disgruntled, but not in the least upset.

"So, you've made the first show of aggression by taking our brother captive when he was under your roof by invitation?"

"He came into another club's territory willingly. No one forced him here. By putting himself in our hands knowing your club had our property and our drugs, he put himself in danger. You either give us back what you took or your man here is the payment."

"That your final say on the matter?"

Crow obviously thought he had the upper hand. His grin widened. "It is."

Torpedo looked around him at the armed men in the room before meeting gazes with Arkham. "Is there anything we can do or say to change your mind?" That was the last warning. Everyone on Bones' team knew it.

"Give me back my drugs. Or pay me for them."

Torpedo sighed. "Then I'm afraid we're at an impasse."

"I guess we are," Crow said, his grin widening. He nodded at his men holding Arkham. One of them raised a handgun, cocked it, and pointed it at Arkham's head. The second Crow nodded his head at his man the second time, the order to execute Arkham, the gunman's head exploded. Arkham kicked out, knocking the second guard off balance and into the wall so hard, the man stumbled through the drywall, getting tangled in the wooden slats of the wall.

Sword and Viper took up positions around Torpedo while pulling out their own guns. The silencers made them a bit awkward and barrel heavy, but the Bones men were still faster and better than the Black Reign members. Sword winged two of the men he'd pegged as the most significant threat, following up to kill one of them. The second ducked behind a couch. Sword turned his attention to the men around them. Arkham had freed himself and had taken another two men out with his bare hands before retrieving a knife from his boot and a gun from one of the men he'd dropped. Viper and Torpedo had each wounded or killed more than one of the men closest to them, including wounding Crow. The Black Reign president screamed out orders even as he retreated behind his men.

Another gunman's head seemed to disintegrate as one of the men from Salvation's Bane unleashed the big .50-caliber sniper rifle a second time. The gun was designed to shoot through concrete to reach its target. Any living thing it hit, it destroyed. The effect on morale for Black Reign was devastating. Crow's men fled in all directions, some dropping their own weapons in surrender before running for cover.

Crow snarled, his own gun in hand. He aimed at Torpedo. Shots from the suppressed sniper rifles of the Salvation's Bane men hit with a sickening thud. Two rounds. A half-second apart. Both hit Crow's middle, ripping his body in half. Blood splattered the walls and the men surrounding him, pooling on the floor in a grotesque display of raw power on the part of Bones.

The whole fight lasted less than three minutes, but Black Reign was in chaos. Women screamed and fled, trying to find shelter. A couple of the men tried to stand their ground, but soon realized it was a fight they couldn't win. Through it all, only a couple of the Black Reign members got off shots. Their guns were the only sounds that echoed through the night, other than the lingering screams of both patched members and everyone else with Black Reign. They were in the middle of an urban area, so it was likely the police were on their way. If so, there was a bloodbath for them to witness.

With Crow dead, that left Handlebar as president until the club could either confirm or replace him. Right now, the man looked like he was going to be sick. "You… you just…" Handlebar looked at Torpedo, disbelief and shock stamped all over his face. "You can't do that!"

"Why not? He was going to kill -- no, execute -- my man. Arkham had his hands tied behind his back. We defended ourselves. Not that anyone will ever know. I doubt you're interested in the law investigating any more than we are."

"This is war! Do you hear me?" The man was rapidly losing any fear he had. Or, more likely, he was afraid of looking weak in front of his brothers. After all, a club in Kentucky would be much harder to war with than a local club. Anything he promised Bones in this moment would quickly be set aside in the face of taking care of their dead and dealing with their supplier. Undoubtedly, they were getting pressure from someone to deliver payment. They'd still have to deal with Bones, but they would have time. Sword could practically see the wheels turning in Handlebar's mind.

Torpedo stalked up to the other man, getting right in his face. He had to stoop because Handlebar was at least a head shorter than Torpedo. "No. It's not. You're gonna to get rid of your dead, then move your operation out of Bones territory. Consider the Oxy Highway through Somerset closed."

"You can't dictate to us! We'll kill every one of you hillbilly motherfuckers!"

"Down, Handlebar." A man emerged from the back of the club, immaculately dressed in an expensive-looking three-piece suit. Not a hair out of place, the man looked like he he'd just stepped out of the pages of a magazine. He had a thick head of jet-black hair and light-earthen-toned skin. Though he looked Hispanic, he had a slight English accent. "You've already been rude to your guests. Further threats only incite more violence."

Sword's attention was now squarely on the newcomer. This guy was more than he seemed. A man of his obvious wealth had to be completely stupid to enter a club like this without muscle. Which meant there was muscle every-fucking-where.

"You seein' this, Trucker?" Sword asked quietly. He had a bad feeling.

"Data's doing computer stuff with him. Says it will take him a few minutes to get any information."

"I don't think we have a few minutes." Sword's heart started pounding, his adrenaline kicking in. There was no indication whatsoever, but he knew in his gut this guy was the real deal. The real threat in the clubhouse at the moment. If Bones and Salvation's Bane hadn't known this guy was here, how many more men like him did Black Reign have? It was possible Sword and his brothers were seriously under-manned.

"I heard from Crow your club is the reason my employer's product is missing." The guy sounded both educated and refined.

"Not missing," Torpedo said, loosening his stance, readying to spring if necessary. "Gone. It's destroyed."

"You really shouldn't have done that." The guy sounded genuinely remorseful. As if what was going to happen next truly pained him.

"Your men shouldn't have gone through our territory without permission."

The man looked thoughtful, as if he were seriously thinking over what Torpedo had said. Then he nodded. "I see your point. Black Reign is nothing if not rude, are they not?" Sword was convinced this guy truly expected an answer. Like he and Torpedo were having a polite conversation about a group of peasants, and they were the lords.

Torpedo was silent for several moments, sizing up the newcomer. "Who are you?"

"You can call me El Diablo. Think of me as your guide to either eternal riches or eternal damnation." The guy simply oozed wealth. From the expensive-looking suit to the Rolex watch, to the three rings and two cufflinks with more diamonds than a jewelry store, the man looked like he could deliver what he so boldly stated.

"I'm sure you are. I also imagine selling one's soul is involved."

The smile from El Diablo turned instantly evil. "You have no idea."

Torpedo opened his mouth to respond, but Data's voice came through their earpieces. "Everyone out! Get the fuck out of there now! And, for God's sake, watch your motherfuckin' backs!"

Sword took up a position in front of Torpedo, switching from his handgun to the rifle hanging across his back. Viper and Sword might be trying to protect their vice president, but the man was watching out for them as sharply as they were watching out for him. If there was trouble, Sword wanted to take out as many as he could. He knew from experience Viper was walking them out, covering the entrance and watching for unfriendlies waiting to ambush. This was where they relied heavily on their brothers from Salvation's Bane. There was no way to get to the underground tunnels, and Sword had a feeling they might be a death trap at this point. With this new unknown and the chance the tunnels weren't exactly safe, he'd rather fight their way out than get caught in a flooding or collapsing tunnel. Or in between the enemy with no way out.

Arkham looked like he might take the motherfucker out, but held himself back, eyeing El Diablo warily. If Arkham gave the guy a pass, there had to be a reason. Still, Arkham looked to Torpedo for direction. If the vice president told Arkham to take this El Diablo out, Sword had no doubt Arkham was up to the task.

"Before you go, I need to give you a message. Tell your president I understand his frustration with Black Reign, but I can't allow rival clubs to take product belonging to my employer under any circumstances. I will require reimbursement."

"What about Magenta?" Handlebar demanded. "That bitch has it comin', and I want her back."

El Diablo addressed Sword, ignoring the acting president of Black Reign. "Consider little Magenta a gift. I'd offer her mother back to you, but the woman didn't seem to understand when it was her time to pay the devil his due."

"What did you do?" Even as he backed away, trying to keep everyone in his line of sight and protect Torpedo on the way out, Sword had to know if there was any way to save Magenta's mother. He'd made Magenta a promise, and he intended on keeping it.

El Diablo waved a hand and a man they hadn't seen before brought a badly beaten woman into the main room and dropped her at El Diablo's feet. The woman mewed pitifully, sounding more animal than human. She didn't even try to move on her own. Though her body was broken, several bones poking through her skin in various places, the woman's face had been untouched, obviously a message. The woman looked so much like Magenta, Sword had no doubt this was her mother. The man who'd brought her in took out his phone and took several pictures of the woman, documenting her injuries. Lastly, he brushed her hair from her face, almost tenderly, before taking a final snapshot.

"Sword, meet Magenta's mother, Ginger. My man will send those photos to your president as proof of her identity. Magenta will be able to confirm it's her. Ginger used to be Crow's. Unfortunately, because Crow's men lost their cargo, this poor woman paid the price." El Diablo grin was an evil slash across his face. Sword didn't question how the man knew his name. He got the feeling this guy had known exactly what he was walking into and had prepared accordingly. If they got out of this without losing anyone, it would either be because El Diablo wanted them to, or because they'd gotten extremely lucky. "She was chosen for more than one reason, though. First, she had her own debts to pay, but the only thing you need to be concerned about is your own debt. Tell Cain I will pay him a visit in two weeks. Because he had every right to defend his territory, I'll give him that time when I normally would simply punish swiftly without warning. If he pays the three hundred thousand dollars my employer's shipment was worth, I'll spare your Magenta. Otherwise..." He trailed off, reaching down to caress Ginger's face. El Diablo knelt beside her, kissing her cheek gently before letting his hand slide ever so slowly to her chin. A sharp crack rang out as Ginger's neck snapped under one swift jerk of El Diablo's hand.

Chapter Eight

"Stash the RV," Torpedo bit out into his helmet mike as they raced back to Trucker and Magenta. "I want everyone ready to leave in fifteen minutes." Sword had never been one to run away from a fight, but he needed more information. Whatever Data had found out on this El Diablo wasn't good. But, given the nature of their work with Cain's paramilitary mercenary-for-hire business, it took more than a simple badass to trigger any of their danger instincts. This guy pinged all over the place.

"We've got your RV," Havoc said. "We can park it at our compound. I'll get you a truck to take back to Kentucky. Once this blows over, we'll swap again."

"Sounds good. Can you escort us to your place? I wouldn't ask, but Sword has Magenta, and they've threatened her."

"You don't need to explain. I'll get Thorn to authorize an escort for you back to Kentucky if you want. I doubt it will be a problem."

"Take him up on it, Torpedo." Sword couldn't keep the order from slipping out. The vice president wouldn't like it, but he couldn't take a chance with Magenta's life. "Whoever this guy is, he's bad news. He might keep his word, and he might be tryin' to get us to lower our guard."

"I'm not stupid, Sword," Torpedo snapped. "We'll take any backup your president wants to send. I suggest you guys prepare here, too. This guy means business."

"Thorn's already on it. He's been listening in for this very reason." Havoc flanked the group as they pulled into the area where the RV was nestled, waiting in hiding. The second they pulled in, Trucker emerged, AK-47 in hand like he was expecting trouble.

"Data sent me the info on this El Diablo character," Trucker said when the bikes were shut down. "He's a ghost. Hired muscle for every major cartel in the world."

"What the fuck's he doing chasing after three hundred thousand dollars in drug money? Seems a bit beneath him."

"We'll figure it all out when we're back in our own territory with the whole club. By that time, I'm sure Data will have more for us."

Sword was glad Torpedo shut down any debate. Discussing this here would make him crazy. To say nothing about the twelve- to thirteen-hour ride home. He'd hoped to have at least a few hours to rest, but that wasn't happening.

"Let's get this RV back to Palm Beach. Once there, we'll figure out ridin' arrangements." Torpedo directed the group with as much ease as Cain always did. It was like they were in the field on a mission. They followed Torpedo's orders as easily as they did Cain's. Sword took some measure of comfort in that familiarity. His brothers were surrounding him. They'd help him get Magenta to safety, then they'd figure out the rest of it.

Once the RV had been swapped for an F-250 and the covered bed loaded with their gear, Sword talked Magenta into riding with Trucker until they were out of Florida. He promised her after that, he'd put her on the bike with him. She hadn't protested, but then he hadn't really expected her to. She didn't fully trust him, though he knew she wanted to. It hadn't been easy parting from her either. Sword had told Magenta her mother was dead, but she hadn't reacted much.

She'd sucked in a breath, but that had been it. Magenta blinked rapidly for a few seconds and then finally murmured, "Thanks for telling me."

Even as they sped up the highway, Sword counted down the miles until she had those slim arms wrapped around his waist again. If he was going to win her over, it would be on the bike. She seemed like she felt as free on it as he did. Besides, with her in danger, he liked knowing she was near. As much as he trusted his brothers, no one could keep her safe like he would.

Instead of taking the more direct route up Interstate Seventy-Five, they decided to cross Florida to the western coast, staying off the interstates. It added a few hours to their journey, but was necessary to give them a chance at knowing if they were being followed. They made it to a little town just south of the Georgia border called Monticello before stopping. It was late afternoon. Torpedo called a halt at a roadside motel.

"We'll get back underway tonight. Be ready to leave at oh-three-hundred."

Sword wasted no time snagging Magenta's hand and pulling her into their room.

"Come here," he growled. Before she could protest, Sword pulled her into his arms and found her mouth with his. Not just into his arms. He surrounded her with his embrace and held her as tightly as he could, needing her to know he'd never let her go but unable to say the words.

He knew he was an ass for doing this. Hell, the girl had probably had more men than he cared to think about do the exact same thing. The thought only fueled his anger and lust because it fueled his fear. Fear of himself and what he'd do to any man who hurt this woman.

When Magenta gasped out a little whimper, he slid his tongue into her mouth, tasting her fully. He kissed and kissed her, needing the contact. Needing the beautiful woman he'd somehow connected with despite the darkness inside him.

Her fingers curled in his shirt, but she didn't push him away. She didn't hold him to her either. Sword backed her against the door, gripping her thigh and pulling her leg up around his hip. Though she didn't seem to know what to do with him like this, she still kissed him. Greedily. Nearly as hungry for him as he was for her. Her little tongue darted inside his mouth, following his retreat until she moaned into him. God, he was greedy for the taste of her! He wanted her abandoned. Though he knew she was skittish -- and rightly so -- he could tell there was a little powder keg inside her waiting to be unleashed by the right man.

Both of them were breathing hard when Sword finally pulled back to look at Magenta. Her blue eyes were glazed and wide with shock. There was a wild look of either fear or excitement in them. He couldn't tell. That look was the only thing that allowed Sword to temper his aggression.

"Don't you give me that look, Magenta. I'm not going to do anything you don't want me to."

"Why did you kiss me, then?"

He kissed her again, a hard pressing of his mouth, but not the sexually aggressive action of before. "You will not make me believe you didn't want to kiss me back. Not with the way you move beneath me. Because I can't help myself," he confessed. "I thought I could, but I can't."

"I'm not a whore." Magenta's voice was hardly above a whisper, but Sword felt her words straight to his soul.

"Never, Magenta. Never. Not for me. Not for anyone else." He had to shake his head to clear it. "God! Don't you fuckin' feel it? I'm burning up!"

She looked at him for a long time, searching his face. His eyes. Sword knew what she saw. He was a killer. A man who took what he wanted. How could she possibly want a man like him?

Finally, she nodded. "I do feel it. So intense I want to let it consume me! I'll take what you're offering. However long it lasts."

Sword didn't waste another moment. He lifted Magenta in his arms, urging her to wrap her legs around his waist, and walked them to the bed. He laid her down gently, following her down to cover her body with his.

"I say when it's over, Magenta."

"I won't cling," she said, shaking her head slightly. "I just want to experience what it's like to really want a man like I want you in this moment."

"I want you to cling," he said. "But only to me."

"And when you tell me to leave?" Her eyes were wide, a mixture of desire, fear, and -- dare he believe -- hope.

"I'm asking for your trust, girl. Unconditional trust. I'll take care of you and protect you, but in return I want you to believe in me."

She stared up into his eyes for long moments. So long, Sword thought she might balk and push him away. Then, finally, she nodded. It was slight, but there.

"Say it, girl. Say you'll trust me to take care of you." He was a bastard for demanding she give him this, but he was doing it, anyway. If he let her think about it, let her take her time getting to know him, she would pull away and leave the safety of the club and cut him out of her life.

"I will. I do. I trust you, Sword." Before he could continue kissing her, however, she placed her hand on the side of his face. "Please don't break my heart."

"Never, my beautiful girl."

Sword pressed his body against her, letting feel his erection against her belly. It was thrilling when she lifted her arms to slide around his neck, pressing her breasts against his chest. She opened her mouth and let him inside, lapping gently at him even as he swooped inside to take what he needed.

Not wanting to wait any longer, Sword gathered the hem of her shirt and whipped it over her head. She wore no bra and, truly, she didn't need one. Her breasts were small but rounded, the nipples stiff and the palest pink. Her body was small, her skin pale. The bruises she'd suffered stood out starkly, an offensive reminder of all she'd suffered. Sword had seen all this before, but now, in this moment, it seemed worse. It was also a reminder he had to be gentle with her. Not take her with all the passion he needed to.

He knelt before her, wrapping his arms around her back before taking one breast into his mouth and pulling strongly. She cried out, threading her fingers through his hair. But she wasn't satisfied to simply feel what he was doing to her. When he let go of one breast to latch on to the other, she clawed his shirt up his back to pull over his head.

That was all Sword needed to know. She found his earlobe and sucked it between her lips, nipping gently.

"You're asking for it, girl," he warned. "Need you too bad for you to do that."

"Need you, too," she whimpered.

He pulled at the waist of her pants the same time she pulled at the button of his jeans. Magenta lifted her hips to help him get her sweats. He shoved his jeans and boxer briefs off his hips before lying on top of her. The skin at her neck was sweet with a light sweat as she squirmed beneath him. Her arms wrapped around his body, gripping his lower back.

It was tempting to just sink into her heat, to do what they both wanted. Instead, he slid down her body, trailing his lips over her belly. He stopped at her belly button to swirl with his tongue once before going lower.

Magenta's body trembled under his touch. Her fingers slid to his shoulders, gripping and kneading as she whimpered with every touch of his lips, teeth, and tongue. Had a woman ever been this so alive in his arms before? Had he ever wanted one to be? This was no feigned passion. This was need, pure and simple. She panted, whimpering her need even as he growled his.

When he reached the top of her sex, kissing the bare mound with a reverent press of his lips, she cried out sharply, her fingers digging into his hair, pulling his scalp. When he would have gone lower, she held him, whimpering. Her hands trembled, her body erupting in sweat.

Sword looked up at her, meeting her blue eyes with his steady gaze. Gradually, she released her grip and nodded. Never looking away from her, Sword swiped her clit with the flat of his tongue.

* * *

Magenta didn't know what to think or do. Never had her body come alive like it was now. She'd known this moment would come, but she hadn't expected to want it this much. Everything inside her yearned for the man stroking her body to such a fevered pitch. There was no pain. No threats if she didn't please him. In fact, he hadn't made her touch him at all. What he was doing, he did to her. There was nothing but pleasure in his touch.

Sword curled his arms around her thighs and fastened his mouth over her pussy. It was her first time, the sensations unfamiliar and almost devastating. Even as she arched her back, planting her feet on the mattress to thrust her pelvis at him for more, tears sprang to her eyes. This was something like she'd never even dreamed of. No pain. No humiliation. She tried to check her responses with little success, not wanting him to get the wrong idea about her, but it was impossible. The best part was how he seemed to revel in her wantonness, not condemning her for it.

"My girl likes this," he said, his voice rumbly, vibrating her clit with every word. "Good. I could do it all night. Love your taste…"

The feel of his lips and tongue on her was like fire and silk. He sucked at her lips and clit, wringing moans and whimpers from her in abundance. Magenta could feel moisture leaking from her cunt only for him to lap it up like a cat with cream. Where before she'd had twinges of pain from the beating she'd taken, now her body was alive with pleasure. She didn't even realize she was keening loudly until Sword crawled up her body and silenced her with a deep kiss. Which was its own surprise. She tasted herself on him. With every stroke of his tongue, every slide of his lips over hers, her own honeyed essence was given back to her so her taste mingled with his.

He held himself over her for several moments, stroking the damp hair at her temples from her face. Sword seemed to be looking for something. Needing something from her. A response of some kind. Magenta was so confused, she didn't know what to say or do. Her hips continually rocked against him, something she found she had little control over.

Finally, he nodded before pushing off her slowly. Once on his feet beside the bed, he kicked off his jeans and underwear. From his wallet, he pulled out two condoms. One he tossed to the nightstand, the other he tore open and used to sheathe himself. Magenta tried not to look at his cock, not wanting anything from her past to color this moment. It was special to her in so many ways. Not the least of which was because of the man climbing back on the bed between her legs.

Slowly, deliberately, Sword let his full weight settle on her. His cock was trapped between them instead of inside her, but he seemed to have a reason, so she said nothing. Again, he kissed her, this time trailing his lips down her jaw to her throat.

"Are you sure you want this? It's your choice as much as mine, and I never want to do something you don't want."

That courtesy more than anything else told Magenta this was a different man than she'd ever known. This was a man who could be her hero if she let him. Was he the white knight in shining armor in fairytales? Not in the least. This man was a killer. Darkness filled him to his very soul. Only his honor kept him from being like the brutal men in Black Reign, but she knew he'd keep his word as surely as she knew her own name. He was exactly the type of man who'd be able to keep his promise to keep her safe because he was just as determined and ruthless as the men who would hunt her.

"I'm sure. I need it, Sword. Please."

"I wanted to wait, but the fight… the violence…"

"I know. I don't want you to wait."

When he still hesitated, she reached between them, shifting her body so she could tuck his cock against her entrance. Sword closed his eyes tightly as he wrapped his arms around her. He'd done it several times, and Magenta loved the feel of his body completely surrounding her. It felt like a layer of protection between her and the rest of the world. Like, as long as he held her, no one could ever hurt her again.

A defeated groan sounded from somewhere deep inside Sword's chest, vibrating all the way through her as he slid forward in a slow, hesitant movement. He seemed to still be at war with himself over what to do.

"You've defeated me, woman," he admitted before withdrawing and sliding deep once again. "So good. So hot and tight I never want to leave!"

Magenta rested her heels on his calves. With every thrust forward he made, she used the leverage to lift herself to meet him. Her movements seemed to encourage him as he moved faster and faster, thrusting harder though he was careful of her battered body.

"You fuckin' tell me if you hurt, Magenta," he bit out at her ear. "I don't want anything for you but fuckin' pleasure."

She had to smile at his harsh words. Nothing about Sword was soft or tender. She thought he wanted there to be, but she was fine with him just the way he was. "It's wonderful, Sword. Don't stop! Please!"

Wonderful sensations swamped her quickly. There was no fighting what she'd never faced before. Sex had never been like this. Wanted. Welcomed. Needed. Something was driving her toward an unknown abyss. Every movement he made pushed her farther in that direction. Every stroke of his hand aided in her surrender to it. It struck her then that this was what women sought from sex. This was how they wanted to feel when they let another have their body.

She was just about to fall over that cliff into an unknown world when Sword shifted his weight, raising up to brace himself on one arm as he held her close with the other. His hand slid down to her ass, guiding her movements while he looked into her eyes.

"You're staying with me, girl," he commanded. "You're coming with Bones to the clubhouse, then you're staying with me." Confused, she tried to ignore him, tried to force him to continue his mastering of her body, but he was having none of it. "Say it!"

"I'm staying with you." She looked up at him knowing he could see her bafflement. "I thought we already decided that?"

"I said when it was over. I'm telling you now it will never be over, Magenta. Do you understand me?"

"No! I don't!" The admission was torn from her in nearly a wail. "I can't think like this!"

"You want to come? Then tell me you understand!" Gone was the gentle lover, the man who was so careful of her battered body. In his place was that ruthless man she knew would protect her to the death. He was declaring his possession of her with her in a very vulnerable position, getting what he wanted by any means necessary.

Magenta whimpered, her chin quivering as she verged on tears. Not because she was scared or hurt, but from frustration. He'd left her hanging on the precipice of something so wonderful and beautiful she knew she'd forever need it like she might need a drug, only to keep it from her.

"Why do this now? Why not finish me first?"

"Because I fuckin' want you that much! Not lettin' you say no, and I'm fuckin' holdin' you to it!"

"Sword!" The possessiveness in his voice pushed her over the edge. She screamed her pleasure, digging her nails into his arms and shoulders. She thrashed beneath him as a searing wave of heat pulsed through her entire body, centered on where they were joined. A hard spasm clamped down on her, seeming to pull him into her body so he couldn't get away from her. Couldn't leave her needy cunt.

"Say it, girl! Say you're mine!" His hand was in her hair, tightening into a hard fist, the little bite of pain adding to her pleasure in a way she'd never imagined. It was a dark pleasure -- one she hadn't expected and never would have experienced if she hadn't known how good he could make her feel. It was a little terrifying, but more thrilling than she could have ever imagined.

"I am," she gasped. "Yours!"

The second the words left her mouth, Sword pounded into her, pushing the boundaries of civil sex and nearing something akin to madness. He growled, taking her hard even as he held her tightly to him. Several seconds later, she felt him thicken, his shaft stretching her just before he roared to the ceiling, emptying himself into the condom. Never separating their bodies, Sword rolled them over to their sides. He still had his arms wrapped tightly around her, his breathing as ragged as hers.

There was a knock at the door, angry and loud. Sword gave a vicious snarl before gently pulling out of her. "You OK, baby?" She nodded, not knowing what to do now that it was over. He kissed her gently once before standing and covering her with the bedspread. Then he tossed the condom in the trash and stalked to the door where someone still pounded angrily.

Sword didn't bother to cover his nakedness, just flung open the door to meet the angry face on the other side. "What the fuck do you want?"

The man standing outside jumped back a couple of steps. Magenta couldn't blame him. Sword was a big man, tall and all tattooed muscle. He looked exactly like what he was. A man not to be fucked with.

"I -- uh, that is," the man cleared his throat. "Nothing." Before the man could say anything else, Sword slammed the door in his face and turned the deadbolt before sliding the chain into place.

He stood there looking at her. Then he sighed.

"What the fuck am I gonna to do with you?"

"I thought you had that all figured out," she said. Unexpectedly, she felt a stirring of happiness. She hadn't exactly grown up in the club life, but she'd been there long enough to know there were men who took ownership of their women very seriously.

"I do," he said. "I have a feelin' you're gonna to be a handful, though."

"That a bad thing?"

"No. Keeps me on my toes. Roll over," he commanded. "Want to see your back and legs. I was hard on you. Didn't mean to be, but I was."

"I felt no pain, Sword. None at all."

"Still want to look at those welts. Some were pretty bad, and you'll need somethin' to keep 'em from hurtin'."

Obediently, Magenta turned over to her stomach. "You sure it's not just so you can get a better look at my ass?"

Sword actually snorted. The first time she'd heard anything resembling a laugh. "Might be."

With a light touch, he traced several of the worst marks over her skin, then spread more antibiotic ointment over them. Any stinging she might have felt faded away seconds later with the soothing coolness his fingers left behind.

"Better?" He bent to kiss her cheek, murmuring the question in her ear. Magenta realized she'd nearly dozed off.

"Yes," she admitted. "Though I didn't really hurt. I didn't even realize there was discomfort at all until you put that stuff on again."

"Good." He urged her up so he could turn down the covers before laying her down again and covering her with the sheet and blanket. "I need to let Torpedo and Cain know what to expect when we get home tomorrow. They need to know you're my ol' lady since I don't have a property patch for you yet."

Magenta's heart soared. "Ol' lady?"

He scowled. "Yeah. That's what I meant by this never ending. You said you understood, and I'm not lettin' you out of this."

She couldn't help the smile tugging at her lips. "Didn't say I wanted out. I just didn't expect something as serious as an ol' lady."

"Yeah, well, don't let it go to your head," he muttered. "Woman will be the death of me." That last was obviously meant for himself. His tone pleased her.

Though he sounded disgruntled, he was very insistent. There was no way he was backing out of this, nor did he take the designation of her as his ol' lady lightly. He meant for her to have the full protection of his club from anyone and everyone who meant her harm.

Instead of feeling the despair she'd often felt in Black Reign before falling asleep, Magenta felt an overwhelming happiness and sense of peace that nearly brought tears to her eyes. "Sword," she called, waiting until he turned to meet her gaze. "Thank you. For everything. For saving me."

He held her gaze. In that moment, Magenta could almost feel his affection. She wasn't ready to call it more than that, but there was more there in his eyes than she'd seen from anyone in her life, including her own mother.

Without a word, he nodded once, then turned away again. Magenta curled her arm under her cheek and closed her eyes. Her last thought before sleep claimed here was to wonder how she'd gotten so lucky for a man like Sword to find her when she needed him most.

Chapter Nine

Had he not been feeling El Diablo breathing down his neck like a hungry wolf, Sword would have happily ridden with Magenta back to Florida. Or to the fucking West Coast and back. The woman truly loved riding on the bike. He'd never met anyone so consumed with the moment when she was behind him. Sometimes she wrapped her arms around his middle and squeezed, her face to his back. Other times, she put her hands in his front pockets and nibbled at the skin at the back of his neck while she petted the tip of his dick through the thin material.

Only two things stopped him. The first was obviously El Diablo. He didn't believe the man would give Bones two weeks. That was a ploy to get the club to relax. Let down their guard. He'd be after them soon and, even though taking off might throw him off their tail, Sword had no desire to face him alone with no one to help him protect Magenta. He was a cocky bastard, but not that cocky. Second? Right before they pulled into the Bones compound, Magenta had slid her arms around him, placing one palm in the center of his chest while the other slid around his hip to fully cup his cock.

Game over.

He needed her in his own house, but his suite in the clubhouse would have to do for now. The little minx knew what she was doing, too. When he turned off the bike and swung his leg over the tank, she giggled. Especially when he scooped her up and took off to the clubhouse.

"If I wasn't afraid you were still hurtin', I'd spank your ass, girl," he growled playfully. To his delight, she continued to giggle.

The door to the compound opened, and Shadow met him. The big man opened his mouth to say something but stopped, shut it, then grinned. "It can wait."

Sword carried her up the stairs to the second floor. All the club members and prospects slept at the clubhouse more often than not if they didn't have families of their own. Those who had no one had their own room, some of them suites depending on their needs and the room available. Sword was glad of it.

Once inside, he locked the door and pulled Magenta to him, kissing her hungrily. "Little witch," he growled. "Teasing me all the way home with your touch and laughter."

"I love riding with you."

"Do you love fuckin' me as well?"

Her breath caught in a little hitch. "Yes," she breathed. "I love it very much."

"Think you could do it again?"

"I think I can manage." Her smile was heavenly. Sword was beat from the long, hard ride, but she'd made it go way too fast and now, he had to have her. It was a necessity.

He separated from her long enough to strip. She did the same, and when they came together again, both were naked and needing. Her little breasts sported pebble-hard nipples straining to his touch, and he could see moisture dripping from her cunt down one thigh.

Pulling her to him, mashing her body against his, was the only thing he could do. Sword wanted to sigh in contentment when her skin slid against his. Her little moans as she rubbed her nipples over his hair-dusted chest were the sweetest music. She met his kiss with a hungry one of her own, sliding her lips delicately over his until he deepened the kiss. She shivered in his arms, clinging to him so sweetly.

Not wanting to wait any longer, Sword lifted her, urging her legs around his waist so he could carry her to the bed. When he did, she let his cock slip between the folds of her pussy, rubbing over him and wetting him with her intimate moisture. She rocked her hips against him, sliding up and down so that his dick rubbed over her clit with every stroke, every movement of her hips and pelvis.

"Good," she breathed. "So good." Magenta nibbled on his ear and neck as he made his way to the bed, taking her down to the mattress and covering her with his bigger body.

"Fuck!" She was driving him insane. The woman had moves that were boggling his mind!

"I love the way you hold me." Her little whimper caressed through him, creating an intimacy he'd never experienced with a woman. "I really do feel safe."

He pulled back to kiss her chin. "I'll always keep you safe, Magenta. If you believe nothin' else, believe that. No matter what, I will make sure no one ever harms you again."

Her smile twisted him up inside, melting a heart he hadn't even known he had. "I also love the way you fuck me. I never knew there was such pleasure. I thought it was all tales women told each other to get through the act."

Sword couldn't help his cocky grin. Even though he wanted to pound every member of Black Reign who'd had her and hurt her, knowing she'd enjoyed his attentions, wanted more of them, eased him somewhat. "Oh, I've got way more to show you, girl. I could keep you locked in here with me for weeks and not scratch the surface. Months."

"Yes," she said, nodding eagerly. "Let's do that."

Sword kissed her even as he laughed at her eagerness. Life with Magenta wasn't going to be dull. There would be moments she'd be skittish, but Sword knew he could always make it better. Maybe not in the moment, but he'd treat her so good she'd come to trust him to know when to pull back. And he would, because she mattered to him.

Needing to be inside her, Sword stretched over her to the nightstand. He snagged a condom from the drawer and rolled it on, discarding the wrapper in the wastebasket beside the bed. Careful not to hurt her, he slid inside her little pussy, savoring the tight glove of her sex. He was rewarded when she arched against him, clinging sweetly to his shoulders and back.

Once inside her, Sword rolled them so he lay on his back with her sprawled over him, his cock fully imbedded.

"Oh!" Her little cry made him smile. She still lay against him, one hand braced on his chest, but seemed baffled as to what he wanted her to do. When he urged her to slide up on him, she gave another cry, this one a little throaty as the new position created a different feelings inside her. "Oh…"

* * *

The new sensations from the foreign position surprised Magenta. His hands rested on her thighs, but he let her set the pace. It took her a few seconds to get the hang of how to move, but once she did Magenta found she could be in control of both their pleasure.

She slid up and down, rocking her hips in a sensual slide. When she figured out how to put a little twist and a snap at the end of her movement, Sword gritted his teeth, and his grip on her thighs tightened. She knew then she had it right.

Over and over she rode him, working to draw out his pleasure and find the limits of hers. Sword's rough hands slid from her thighs to her waist, his big hands nearly spanning her middle. He paused only a moment, and then his hands worked their way up to her breasts, where he cupped her, pulling and tugging at her nipples. Still she moved.

Magenta loved watching Sword's face while she pleasured him. There was an intensity and passion she'd never expected. Her experience with sex before hadn't been more than a man on top of her or behind her shoving inside her until he came. She'd never enjoyed it. Never wanted to enjoy it. Enjoying sex with the men Handlebar sent her to would mean she really was a whore. If she'd wanted the sex they'd forced on her, the horrible treatment and less-than-careful handling of her, it would have been so much worse. She might have done something rash. But this with Sword...

Everything was a new experience. Everything was good and exciting and welcomed with open arms. She loved the way his expression hardened when he was trying to hold on, to not come. She loved that he thought to protect her with the condom he'd used both times. And she loved that he recognized how much she loved riding the bike with him and was willing to give it to her even when they both knew there could be danger. He had surrounded her with every member of Bones and Salvation's Bane, putting them both in the middle of the pack in order to give her what she wanted. He'd insisted they make it out of Florida first, but he'd done it for her. For that alone, she'd do everything she could to give him pleasure.

With a rough growl, Sword sat up, pulling her to him, surging up into her as he wrapped his arms around her tightly. He had a way of doing that every time he hugged her to him, enveloping her in his strong arms. Shifting positions, he turned the tables on Magenta, taking control with an effortless grace that left her breathless. Sword was on his knees sitting back on his heels, moving her in time with his own movements as easily as if she weighed nothing. The casual display of power thrilled Magenta beyond belief, triggering her orgasm.

With a shrill cry, Magenta came in a wet rush of heat. She clung to Sword, needing everything he had to give her. Giving him every part of her without reservation. She trusted him with her life, her heart. In that moment, she was all in, and knew she would be for better or worse. She'd given Sword her heart.

She screamed his name, arching her back to give him access to her breasts. The need for him to possess all of her was there, open for the taking. As she knew he would, Sword wasted no time taking what she offered. His mouth found one nipple and he sucked, prolonging her pleasure.

The moment she felt him swelling inside her, Magenta locked her arms around his neck, pulling herself upright and finding his mouth with hers. She thrust her tongue inside, kissing him with all the feelings inside her she either couldn't name or was afraid to put into words. Maybe she'd latched on to him because he seemed to be the first decent man she'd ever met. Maybe it was his magnetism. Or, perhaps, they were just drawn to each other with some kind of cosmic force neither understood. All Magenta knew was that she needed him with her. Inside her. Beside her. And, when the time called for it, in front of her.

Sword was all that and more. Right this moment, he was giving her enough pleasure to last a lifetime.

When it was over, when they were both finally spent, Sword kissed her gently. He trailed kisses from her jaw to her neck and back to her lips. His hands trailed a soothing caress over her back and buttocks.

"Are you OK?" His question no longer surprised her. Though he was wild with her, he was mostly careful. When he wasn't, he always soothed her afterward.

"I'm wonderful," she replied. Even to herself she sounded drowsy. Sated.

"Good. I'll clean up and join you. We can rest for a few hours before we meet with Cain. He'll want a full report from me, what he hasn't gotten from Torpedo, but he'll give us time to settle in." Sword was glad Magenta had already positively identified the woman in the pictures El Diablo had sent to Cain, though he hadn't told her who'd actually killed Ginger. He didn't want her to go with him when he faced the president. Not because he was afraid he'd get dressed down, but Cain could be a bit intimidating at the best of times. Magenta had been through enough for the time being.

"Is he going to be mad at you for bringing me with you?" Magenta hated how insecure she sounded, but there it was. Perhaps she'd always have a part of her that felt that way, but she hoped she could get past it to be the woman Sword deserved.

"Cain? Hell no! You're exactly where you should be. You're my woman. The club protects each other. We all protect our women and children. We're one big family, and we have each other's backs. Black Reign and El Diablo will come no matter what. Better you're with us than on your own. Even if you weren't my woman."

"El Diablo?" Magenta's stomach clenched in fear and she thought she might throw up.

"You know of him?" Instantly, Sword was all business.

"He's bad news, Sword. One of the few things my mother warned me about was El Diablo."

"Apparently, he's muscle for the actual owner of the shit Black Reign was sellin'. Though, what we can't figure out is why he's involved with such a miniscule amount. Three hundred thousand dollars is pocket change to the type of people this guy works for."

"All I know is my mother knew him from before she brought us to Black Reign. I heard her arguing with someone when I came home from school. There was a handsome man sitting in our living room. He said nothing, just sat there watching Ginger intently. I didn't think he'd even noticed I was there, but he was the one to greet me."

"How long ago was this?"

"Six years ago. My sophomore year."

Sword winced slightly, muttering, "I'm so fucked." Then he shook his head. "What were they talking about?"

"Honestly? I'm not completely sure. Looking back, I think she might have gotten El Diablo to do something to my grandparents. It was only a couple weeks later they were in the car accident that killed them."

"So, possibly, he was coming for payback from her anyway." Sword looked like he was absorbing every scrap of information she was giving him and considering it carefully. "What else?"

"I never saw him again after that, though he spoke to me at length. Nothing out of the ordinary. Just how I was doing in school. What subjects I liked. Did I play sports. That sort of thing. He was very polite but not overly friendly. He told me that, if I continued to do well in school, I'd get scholarships to college. I could be anything I wanted to be. I could leave Florida and never look back, if that's what I wanted. Before he left, I heard him tell my mother she didn't have much time and that he would be back. I have no idea what he meant, but I'm sure it had everything to do with what you said happened before you guys left the Black Reign compound. He was there to collect a price from her for whatever happened six years ago." She took a breath, knowing she was rambling, but the memory was distant by now. She knew she needed to give Sword as much information as she could. Let him figure it all out because she couldn't. "I asked her who the man was. She told me he was the devil. El Diablo. She said the only thing I needed to know about him was that he was evil. He'd kill me without a moment's hesitation if I ever came across him. I remember thinking that everything they'd taught us in school about being aware of strangers and just because someone was nice to us didn't necessarily mean they were nice finally made sense."

"But what could be worth the amount of money this man deals in that he caught up with your mother now?"

"Maybe it was the combination of things? Three hundred thousand dollars plus whatever my mother owed him."

"Maybe." Sword frowned, shaking his head. "Doesn't add up, but we've got nothing else." He looked at Magenta again. "How long after that visit did you say it was before your grandparents died?"

"Just a couple of weeks. Maybe a month. I can't remember the exact time frame."

"And how long after that before your mother took up with Black Reign?"

"Immediately. Crow moved her in, but didn't make her his ol' lady for another year. It was the end of my junior year when he did because I wasn't allowed to go back for my senior year."

Sword's jaw clenched, but he only nodded once to acknowledge her. He stood and walked toward the bathroom before glancing at her over his shoulder. "Don't go anywhere. I'll be right back."

As if she could go anywhere. Magenta was bone-tired. She'd slept better than she ever had the night before, safe for the first time in a very long while. But the emotional turmoil and the long bike ride -- no matter how enjoyable -- had taken its toll on her body. She was nearly asleep when Sword crawled into bed with her. She let him pull her against him and wrap her up in his strong arms. God, she loved that! Sleeping with another was the most vulnerable position she could imagine, but it felt natural with Sword. Right.

With a sigh and a kiss to his chest, Magenta let sleep have her, safe in the arms of a man to rival even El Diablo.

Chapter Ten

Two weeks was an eternity for a club like Bones to prepare for an attack. They had the place sealed off in twelve hours, locked down like Fort Knox within forty-eight, and every single member of the club, including four from Salvation's Bane who'd escorted them from Florida, at the ready. Sword had no idea exactly what they were preparing for, but they weren't taking chances with the women and children in their care.

During that time, not only did Sword help his club prepare for war, but he got to know his woman. Magenta was nothing he could have ever imagined. She was giving, loving, and so passionate she rivaled his own appetites. She was hesitant at first, unsure of her footing or what she really wanted. Sword knew he probably should have backed off and let her come around on her own, but he was a bastard. Wanting her was a craving inside him he couldn't fight. Her light filled him every time he looked at her, beckoning him. Keeping her was a must. As a result, he seduced his way into her life, pleasuring her in every way he could, giving her anything she desired until his brothers were laughing at him and the women were sighing over Magenta.

The night before the end of the two weeks El Diablo had given them was the night Sword knew Magenta was his. She not only initiated sex the first time that night, but several times. By the morning, Sword was worn out and happier than he could ever remember being. Magenta had passed out cold draped over his naked body while he sifted her long, silky hair through his fingers.

His phone chimed and he reached for it, careful not to disturb Magenta.

Group text from Bohannon. *Heads up. Incoming right to the front gate.*

As prepared as the club was, Sword wasn't ready. Wasn't ready to give up this time with Magenta. Wasn't ready for her to see how close to danger she still was. She was protected, but he didn't want her to feel like she had to rely on the club for protection. He wanted her to feel strong on her own.

Carefully, he extracted himself, leaving her hugging his pillow, all that pale hair fanning out over her naked body. Very gently, he pulled the covers higher over her, wishing he could wrap her up in a protective cocoon until this was all over and El Diablo and his men were gone.

He sent an acknowledging text before leaving the room to meet his brothers. Before he left, Sword placed a gentle kiss to Magenta's temple. Mama and Pops, the self-appointed parents of the club, would be up after her before they locked everyone in the basement. No need to wake her just yet.

Once in the church, their meeting hall, Cain leaned over the table where Data was scrolling through a tablet, giving him information as they planned their defense. Sword stood by, checking weapons with Bohannon, making sure all was ready.

"Not much for being on the defensive," Bohannon commented.

"Don't think we will be long." Sword nodded in Cain's direction. "Look at his face."

Bohannon glanced at the president, raised an eyebrow, and then nodded. "Nope. Not long at all."

Cain was angrier than Sword could remember seeing him in a long time. It had been building since they'd gotten back, but he had worked up a good pissed-as-hell. Which didn't bode well for anyone going up against Bones.

"Bohannon," Cain called. "Deadeye, Goose, and Shadow need to set up above the compound. I want one on the room, two at flank."

"On it," Bohannon acknowledged with a glance at Sword.

"Mama and Pops have the children and our women in the basement where they will stay," Cain continued. "Arkham, I want those two nephews of yours with Clutch at the door to the basement. Anyone gets near that door who's not affiliated with Bones and they don't kill 'em, I'll be skinnin' someone alive. You make sure they understand I mean fuckin' business."

Arkham acknowledged Cain with a nod. Bohannon raised an eyebrow at Cain. The president shrugged. "They either gotta shit or get off the fuckin' pot. Arkham knows that. I think you made your point when they let your woman slip out on them. They've been better."

"Yeah. Better compared to the train wreck they were before. No place to go but up."

They all had a little chuckle at that, which lowered the tension to a more manageable level. Cain was definitely in a snit. Not that Sword blamed him. The entire club was in jeopardy in their own fucking territory. Danger they accepted. But not on their home turf. That was their safe haven. El Diablo was about to feel the wrath of a pissed-off bunch of ex-military bikers. Sword could almost feel sorry for the guy.

"I know I haven't shared all the details about El Diablo with you. Frankly, Data had a hard time finding much on the guy. What he did find suggests the man is a sociopath, killing as he sees fit, whenever he sees fit.

As Sword's woman suggested, he's a high enforcer for every major mafia and cartel in the world and has been for the better part of two decades. Which means he's fuckin' dangerous." Cain paused, looking at each of them. "Watch each other's six. You all know your positions. High alert. Every one of you is highly trained. You know what's blusterin' and what's real. This is a use-your-best-judgment situation. You think there is a reasonable chance we're fixin' to get shot at, you kill the motherfuckin' threat. No questions asked."

The instructions were highly unusual. It not only showed how much Cain trusted every single man in Bones and what he was capable of, but how pissed off he really was. It was basically an open license to kill the enemy. The only person any of them had to answer to was his own conscience. They all understood. It was what Sword was hoping for. He'd take out this El Diablo, bury him in the mountains where even God would have a hard time finding him.

Sword looked around the room. His brothers. Every single one of them was family. Every single one of them would band together to protect every person associated with Bones. He glanced at the hallway entrance, the one leading deeper into the clubhouse. Mama entered the room and quietly went to the weapons and ammunitions table, organizing ammo so the guns that would be emptied quicker than others would have ready reloads. The thing about Mama and Pops was that Pops was the nurturer. Mama was the real threat. Well, until anyone threatened Mama. Then Pops wasn't so nurturing.

A minute later, everyone seemed ready. No one moved, looking to Cain for direction. Cain nodded once. "Let's do this."

They split up into three groups, each group leaving the clubhouse from a different exit. Low one-two whistles from different areas in the woods surrounding the clubhouse indicated the men hidden there were ready and waiting for trouble. The sound of bikes on the gravel road, the only way in or out of the compound area, rumbled in the distance, the signal trouble was indeed headed their way.

"Look sharp," Sword snapped. "Be ready for anything."

As Black Reign came into view, Sword noticed two very important things. First, the bikes surrounded a black limo that could only be for El Diablo. No self-respecting biker would be caught dead in a cage like that. Second, he only recognized a couple of the bikers riding guard. Handlebar was there as well as a guy named Rycks. Rycks was younger than Handlebar by a good decade, but the man was one of the few Black Reign members who knew what the fuck he was doing. He wasn't flashy and didn't talk much. The only reason Sword had noticed him was because he'd pegged him as the most dangerous man in the room the first time they'd entered the Black Reign clubhouse. He only knew his name by the cut the man wore. There was no officer patch, but he was definitely a fully patched member of Black Reign. None of the other riders in this escort had been in the clubhouse in Florida either time Sword had been present.

Seconds later, the groups stopped. Handlebar revved his engine several times, an obvious show of intimidation, but stopped when none of the others followed suit. He scowled, but said nothing, instead switching off his bike when the others did.

The driver of the limo got out and opened the back passenger door. El Diablo stood, adjusting the cuffs of his shirtsleeves under the suit he wore. As before, diamonds and gold adorned his fingers and the cufflinks. Strangely, it wasn't gaudy as it should have been, but rather a casual display of his wealth.

"Cain," he called to their president. "So good to see you." The guy had the nerve to act like he and Cain were old friends. "I regret we have to meet under such circumstances, but business is business, after all."

"So they say," Cain responded. "We can cut the bullshit. Bones isn't payin' you a dime, and you don't get the girl." Every member of Bones standing at the gate either cocked his weapon or chambered a round, the clicks loud in the silence of the day. Even the birds seemed to have gotten scarce.

"I see," El Diablo said. The man was a cool customer, Sword would give him that. He glanced sideways to where Cain stood beside him. His president didn't give an inch of ground or show any more expression than El Diablo. "Then we are at an impasse."

"Maybe. But I don't believe so."

"Oh, really?" El Diablo's smile didn't reach his eyes. "Why would you say that?"

"Because a man like you doesn't quibble over a mere three hundred thousand dollars. And before you say it's the principle of the matter, a man like you doesn't quibble over a mere three hundred thousand dollars." The sardonic repetition of Cain's previous remark was evident. "You send an underling to make a less-than-finessed example of the fucker who ripped you off."

This time, El Diablo laughed full out, genuine humor in his expression. "My, but you are a treasure. Seems Black Reign stumbled onto the one club in the area with both backbone and brains to back it up." He stepped around the limo door. The driver shut it, standing next to the car with his arms crossed at the wrists in front of him, within easy reach of a gun he carried, but not an offensive gesture. "You're right, of course. I'm not called in for something of this caliber. My interests lie more with the girl."

Sword's hackles rose, and he had to resist the urge to growl and show his teeth at the man. Staying silent was a lesson in restraint.

"Let's hear it." Cain shrugged. "Not that it matters."

"First," El Diablo said, raising a finger into the air, "what are your intentions with little Magenta?"

Cain glanced at him, Sword's permission to talk. "She's mine."

"Yours? By mutual consent or by... invitation from you?"

"If you mean is she with me of her own free will, then yes. She is."

"And you believe you're the man for her?" Sword got a bad feeling. Did this man have some kind of hold on Magenta? Wait...

"She said you knew her mother."

"I did. Let's just say little Magenta was mine before she was yours."

"That may be, but she's made her choice. She stays with me."

"Or what? Are you prepared to die for a woman who doesn't belong to you?"

Sword raised his weapon to point straight at El Diablo. Surprisingly, Handlebar was the only member of Black Reign to counter his threat. "Damned straight. I protect what's mine to the fuckin' death."

"And do your brothers feel the same way? Because, I assure you, if we fight for Magenta, I'll kill every single member of Bones to get to her. Sparing no one."

"We fight for each other," Cain supplied, his voice ringing loud and clear with truth. He aimed his own gun at El Diablo.

"Anything else to say before we start this?" El Diablo sounded almost pleasant. He still hadn't reached for a gun, nor had any of his men. Even Rycks seemed completely at ease. Given the situation, Sword knew there was another shoe to drop.

"Yeah," Sword said, shifting his aim to Handlebar. "Once the shooting starts, I can't concentrate on killing this sorry son of a bitch." Handlebar glanced nervously at El Diablo. Apparently, the man had put the fear of God into him over shooting before given the order. "I want him dead before we kill the rest of you."

El Diablo shrugged. "The man is a rather vile creature, is he not?"

"He hurt Magenta," Sword said. He didn't feel like he owed El Diablo an explanation, but he wanted it clear that he'd remove any threat to her, regardless of the threat to himself.

"Indeed. I've heard all about his exploits. I have another proposition in mind for you, though."

"Oh?" Sword had to hear this.

Instead of answering Sword, El Diablo took out his gun and calmly shot Handlebar in the head. No one in Black Reign moved or in any way lifted a finger to stop El Diablo. In fact, they looked as if they'd been expecting the move. The man calmly put his gun back into his shoulder holster before taking a few slow steps toward Bones. Toward Sword in particular. The man's gaze was glued to Sword's.

"One thing I need to make quite clear, Sword. I've missed much of Magenta's life because of that bitch of a mother of hers. I don't intend to miss any more. I also will not tolerate anyone mistreating her."

Sword opened his mouth but had no idea what to say. Finally, he shook his head. "I'm confused."

"Magenta is my daughter, Sword." The man looked deadly. The El Diablo Data had dug up on the dark web. The killer for hire. The man with no soul. "If you intend to keep her, I will know that she's here because she wants to be. Know that, if you harm one hair on her head, I will hunt you down and make you beg for death." There was no thin veneer of civility about El Diablo now. Where before he'd seemed refined and aristocratic, now he was the devil himself. The threat was clear. What's more, Sword believed him.

"I watched you kill Ginger. Magenta knows it was you who murdered her mother. Even if she wasn't with me because she wanted to be, do you honestly think she'd want to go with you?"

"I told you Ginger had her own debts to pay. Fortunately for me, Crow truly cared for her, though he tried to hide it from everyone. Ginger was going to die, regardless. Punishing Crow gave me reason to drag out her death." The man truly had no soul. Sword saw no regret, only grim satisfaction on his face. "If you must know, the reason for Ginger's death was the same as the reason for Handlebar's death. She hurt Magenta. Perhaps not directly, but she knew the girl was being mistreated and did nothing to protect her. Ginger, as always, was only out for her own well-being."

"Did you kill Magenta's grandparents?" Sword had to know. Whether or not he killed El Diablo depended entirely on the answer to this question.

"It was certainly what Ginger asked of me, but no. I'm guilty of many things, but I do not kill innocents. When I visited Ginger that day, I did so because she reached out to me. She did so under the pretense that she and Magenta were being abused by her parents and needed help. Of course, I offered to take them both away with me. Back to London. But that wasn't what she wanted. Oh, she said all the pretty words, not wanting to be a burden to me, not wanting money from me, she just wanted freedom to live her life and raise our daughter in peace."

"I take it things went sideways?"

"After I left, I investigated the matter. I hadn't told her 'no' outright. Admittedly, my chosen profession isn't exactly mired in good conscience, but even El Diablo has his own rules. My number one rule is that I do not harm the innocent. I'm not above the occasional threat on someone's family if I believe it will get the end result I need, but I've never carried it out unless it's a case like Crow's." The man waved his hand dismissively. "Anyway, once I looked into the matter, and it was easy really, Ginger and Magenta were doing fine. Ginger's parents refused to give her access to Magenta's trust fund, or to extend her already substantial bank account. I told Ginger I was watching her. Taking a teenage girl home with me to raise was out of the question for many reasons, but I told Ginger I'd keep watching. If she failed that girl because of her own greed and lust for power, I'd kill her myself."

"Took you long enough," Sword snapped. "She'd been with Black Reign for six fuckin' years!"

"I'm well aware of that. Circumstances beyond my control made it impossible for me to come for her. It wasn't until the missing drug shipment I was afforded an opportunity. Beneath my notice, usually, but a legitimate reason to be in that territory." When Sword opened his mouth to question that, El Diablo raised a hand in surrender. "Suffice it to say there are many men more powerful than I, and I've made enemies of several. They are not as discerning as I when it comes to killing."

"So, now that we've all got this warm and fuzzy feelin'," Cain drawled, "what do you propose we do now? 'Cause, I gotta tell ya, me and the boys are itchin' for a fight."

"Let me talk to Magenta."

"Not happenin'," was Sword and Cain's immediate reply. Sword glanced at Cain apologetically, but said nothing more.

"I'm here." The subtle feminine voice made Sword want to throw something. Or turn the gun on himself and end it all. Magenta had managed to thwart Mama and Pops as well as the prospects and was even now approaching the group of men. "What do you want to talk about?"

Sword immediately went to her, stopping her forward progress. Arkham moved into Sword's place without hesitation to cover Cain. "Magenta, you need to get back inside." He tried to steer her back to the clubhouse, but she was having none of it.

"You said you wanted to talk," she addressed El Diablo. "If I agree, will you leave Bones alone for good?"

"I have no ill will toward Bones. Never did. The money was an excuse to get into the area to get you out of danger."

"What do you want to know?"

"Only that you're safe and happy." Finally, El Diablo looked as if he'd let his guard down. The superior smirk was gone. In its place was a worried, haggard expression that made Sword actually feel sorry for the guy. This was a man whose only concern was his daughter.

"I am now." She put her hand into Sword's. "Thanks to Sword and Bones. They got me away from Black Reign. Sword and I are together now."

"Are you sure that's where you want to be? You've only been away from your mother for two weeks. Don't you think you need some time to think about all of this?"

"All I know is I feel safe here. I'm still getting to know the ropes and the people here, but they're good to me. There are teenagers here not much older than I was when I first met you. One girl who's a few years younger. She reminds me of me when Ginger first moved us to Black Reign. Only difference is, here, Suzie has a chance at a real life. She's so smart, and everyone realizes she is. They don't beat her down. They encourage her." Magenta smiled, and the whole world seemed to light up. "I like it here. And Sword is so protective of me. He treats me good."

El Diablo glanced up at Sword. "Then I'll leave my daughter in your care." Abruptly, he turned his back and went to the limo, where his driver immediately opened the passenger-side back door. "I'll be in touch. Also, Black Reign is officially under a new president." He spread his hands and smiled. "El Diablo." Sword wanted to kick something. Would this club be a friend or enemy?

"This is Bones territory," Cain said. "You don't run drugs in our territory. You do and expect to lose anything you bring. Men or smack. We don't give second warnings."

"Understood. I'll spread the word that the Oxy Highway through this part of the state is officially closed. Anyone brings anything through here will be on their own."

"Expect you to stay in Florida."

"Unless my daughter needs me, yes."

"Don't forget the fuckin' trash." Cain nodded once at the body of Handlebar. One of the bikes pulled around the group from the back. Surprisingly, it had a small trailer behind it. Two of the Black Reign men wrapped Handlebar's body in a tarp, tying it tightly, and shoved it into the trailer, rolling his bike in after.

El Diablo gave them a small salute before ducking into the car. The rest of the group started up their bikes, and they all left the Bones compound in a trail of dust.

Chapter Eleven

The immediate crisis might be over, but neither Sword, Cain, nor Bohannon let their guard down. They locked the clubhouse down tight the rest of the day. Data had managed to get a tracking device on both El Diablo's car and Rycks's bike, as well as three other of the Black Reign bikes. Small tracer shot from the rooftop had done the trick nicely. Just to be safe, there was round-the-clock security and lights-out after dark. Which was fine with Sword. He had plans with his woman that didn't involve leaving his bed. He could give two shits about the lights.

Now, he lay in bed, her slender body pressed tightly against his as he took her mouth gently. How he managed gentle he didn't know. Even after taking her multiple times a day for two weeks, he was hungry for her. All the damned time. Her squirming against him didn't help matters at all.

As he kissed her, Sword found the tie at the end of her long braid and tugged it free, wanting her hair surrounding him as he surrounded her with his body. She arched into his chest, brushing her breasts against him in an erotic slide, giggling when he growled.

"Little witch."

"Am not," she teased. "I'm just a woman."

"My woman." He nipped her earlobe sharply.

She gasped out, "I am!"

Sword bit her neck gently, then lapped at her with the flat of his tongue. She always tasted good. Fresh morning dew. All woman.

Without warning, she rolled, urging him to his back. When he complied, she ran her lips down his chest to his navel, looking up at him with those big, blue eyes. Even in the dim lighting of the setting sun, he could see them sparkle at him. The woman was up to something.

She settled between his thighs, her soft palm going to his cock and heavy balls. He was already at attention, but her touch made him throb in her hand. He bit back a groan, afraid to encourage her too much lest he come before he was ready.

When she bent her head to his cock slowly, he knew he was in trouble.

"Woman…"

She engulfed the head.

"Ahh!" His sharp cry was punctuated by a sharp jerk of his hips. He wanted to thrust himself deep inside her mouth, but didn't dare, afraid he'd hurt her. She hummed around him, her eyes closing, a look of contentment on her lovely face. She opened her eyes slowly, peering up him. Was the little vixen testing him? She engulfed him again, taking him deep. Sword felt the back of her throat, felt it milking him.

That was all he could take. He pulled her up by her hair, telling himself he needed to be careful with her, but unable to suppress the beast inside him that was hungry for his mate. "Come here, girl," he bit out. She draped over his body like a little cat, finding his mouth with hers. Sword shuddered when he tasted himself on her tongue. "Fuck!" He groaned, as he rolled with her, still lapping at her mouth.

"Sword," she sighed, arching against him.

He wanted to tell her what she meant to him, but had no idea how to express it. Did he love her? He didn't know. As much as he was capable of the emotion, perhaps he did. Romantic love for a woman was a new experience for him. One he was finding uncomfortable, but refused to give up.

He rubbed her neck and chest with his beard, using any means at his disposal to stimulate her. She trembled in his arms, clinging to him so sweetly. He'd intended to eat her out, to drive her mad, but she stopped him. Placing a hand on his face, she brought him in for a kiss, her tongue tangling with his until she bit sharply on his lip.

Sword gasped, pulling back slightly even as his cock jumped, nearly exploding with need. "What are you playing at, girl?"

She slipped her hand between them, gripping his length in her hand to guide him to her entrance. "You're going in bareback, Sword." The sultry rasp of her voice bewitched him, made him so fucking hard he wanted to fill her little pussy good. "You're going to fuck me and come so deep and so hard... All right there inside me."

"Fuckin' hell!" He sank into her, pumped once, then pulled out, knowing he'd never last if he took her in that position.

With a brutal yell, he flipped her onto her belly, pulling at her hips until she was on her knees, ass in the air, chest on the bed. With a savage thrust, he entered her, burying himself to the hilt. They both cried out. Sword began a driving, punishing rhythm, reveling in her cries.

He slid his arms around her middle, pulling her up to her knees in front of him. One hand slid to her breast, squeezing the firm globe and tweaking the puckered nipple. His other hand found her clit and stroked. Still, he fucked her.

"Ah, God! Sword!"

"That's it, baby. Come for me! Can you do that?"

"Yes! Yes!"

When her body clamped down on him, a scream tore from her throat, brutal and anguished. Her body quivered around him. Her nails dug into his ass, pulling her to him when he slowed his thrusts in an attempt to delay his own orgasm. She was having none of it.

"Come with me, Sword," she gasped out. "I need you to come inside me!"

"Fucking hell," he muttered. "Goddamn! Fuck!"

There was no stopping it. Sword felt himself swelling, come rising and threatening to fill her with his hot essence.

Then he did. With a brutal roar, Sword shoved himself inside her as far as he could, clamping her hips to hold her steady while he filled her. Come spilled around them, dripping down their thighs. His balls. Still, he was hard. Needing more of her.

He collapsed with her back on the bed, falling to their sides so he didn't hurt her.

"Are you all right? Did I hurt you?" He was breathing hard as he pressed adoring kisses to her neck and shoulder.

"You know you didn't. I loved every second of what we did."

"Good. Because I want to try that again, now that I've taken the edge off. I wasn't nearly ready for it to end."

Magenta giggled, moving her body around him. He was still buried inside her even though he'd spent himself. His dick pulsed with interest when she slid over him.

"Me neither. I might need a second, though."

"With everything that happened today, I'm not surprised."

"I needed this, Sword." She turned to look up at him, something like love shining in her eyes. He wanted that for himself. Wanted her love. Her heart. "I'm not sure I could have could have survived if you hadn't found me. Then you showed me what making love was."

"Making love?" Sword snorted. "Not sure anyone else would call what we do making love."

"It's how we make love. It's special to me." She reached back to cup his cheek in her hand. "You're special to me."

"Tell me you love me, girl," he demanded before he could censor himself.

She giggled. "Only if you tell me first."

Did he? He thought it over. "I'm not sure I know what love is between a man and a woman," he said seriously. "I know I don't ever want to try livin' without you. I know I'll kill any anyone who tries to hurt you or take you away from me. I know..." He took a breath. "I know I want to be a better man so, maybe, I can deserve you." He kissed her temple. "Is that love?"

"It's our love," she whispered. "It's our love."

Viper (Bones MC 4)

Marteeka Karland

Darcy: I didn't run away from a sadistic stepfather and a mother who wouldn't protect me just to be carted off by some strange man. I fought the son of a bitch. Woulda won, too, except the bastard had help.

Viper's rough around the edges and some kind of badass biker, so there's no way this is going to work out well. Unfortunately, he calls to me on a purely sexual level. Makes my heart race and my body melt just looking at me. It doesn't help he's actually nice to me. He claims to know my dad. My real dad. Says he's been sent to bring me back. I have no idea if I believed him or not. Just don't really have a choice but to go along. At least for now.

Viper: I tracked the cunning little wench for three fuckin' days. In the fuckin' snow. She's good, too. She survived on her own in a hostile environment with only a little trouble. That alone would make me respect for her, but then she had to go and kick me in the balls. Had I not been on the ground in agony, I'd have been turned on beyond belief. Now I've got to figure out how to keep my hands off her so her father won't kill my sorry ass.

It's Christmas Eve, and there's an enemy on our doorstep with a unique gift. One that will leave us all with some hard choices -- Darcy especially.

Chapter One

Winter hung heavy in the hills of Kentucky. One thing Viper hated was winter. Not because of the cold, snow, and ice, but because of the absolute silence in the outdoors. It made hunting that much more difficult. Normally, he enjoyed a challenge, but when the prey was human, there could be nothing to give him away. He'd been on her trail for three days now. There had been no sign of a fire or that she'd sheltered anywhere other than a snow dome she'd built to block the wind and keep in as much of her body heat as she could.

She was good, he'd give her that. He'd been in the service with men who couldn't do what she could, especially given the few resources she had. As far as he could tell, she had nothing but the clothes on her back. One thing was for sure, once he got her back to the Bones compound, she had some explaining to do.

"Anything yet?" Data sounded anxious. And with good reason. Their intel and communications man had only just found out that he had a daughter, and only because her mother had called exactly three days ago -- an hour before Viper and Arkham had been set on her trail -- and informed him. Though the woman had remarried several years earlier, she kept in touch with Data. Why, Viper didn't know. That was Data's story and one he'd have to share with his daughter. Apparently, the only reason his ex had told him about Darcy now was because she'd run off, and her mother was done with the girl. Couldn't deal with Darcy any more. Data's daughter was her daddy through and through. Though Viper had no idea what Darcy had done, it was enough to make her mother and the woman's husband abandon Darcy while the couple and their other two daughters -- not Data's --

went to California on vacation. Data had been livid. Viper had a feeling his next assignment would be to hunt down the girl's mother and stepfather and teach them a lesson.

"I'm just that little bit behind her, brother. Another hour and I should have her, though."

"She's one little girl! You're a big bad Marine sniper! This shouldn't be that fuckin' hard!" Viper raised his eyebrows. Data was normally a by-the-numbers kind of man. He never got excited unless it was warranted. Kind of like when he realized his crew was in the middle of El Diablo's muscle with only one team and minimal backup.

"Relax, brother." Arkham sounded almost bored when Viper knew he was alert and watching as intently as he was. "Girl's wily. Uses the landscape for cover. Even found a snow dome where she slept last night."

"She can't last out there forever with no fire. Rein her in!"

Viper knew when a man was on the edge. Didn't take a genius to know Data was there. "We got this, brother. We'll have her back at the compound by tomorrow." It was a hard promise, but one Viper intended to keep. He ground his teeth. One little girl indeed.

Light was fading in the winter sky. Clouds hung heavily, promising more snow after nightfall if not sooner. Nothing stirred around them. Animals huddled down to wait out the coming storm. Even the evergreen trees were still in the slight breeze. The silence was nearly total.

"Got her," Arkham muttered through his earpiece. "Your four o'clock. She just sat on a fallen log." There was a pause while Viper looked in the indicated direction. "She's done, Viper. I'm headed in."

Sure enough, the girl sat on the log about a hundred yards away. She looked up at the sky, then at her surroundings and put her head in her hands. Yep. She was done.

Viper made his way to her as Arkham came at her from the opposite direction. They were almost on her before she realized she wasn't alone. Immediately she slipped off the log and crouched into a defensive position, grabbing a rock beside her to use as a weapon.

She didn't say a word. Viper expected to see fear in her eyes, and perhaps there was. But mostly what he saw was a cold, hard determination.

"We're not gonna hurt you," Viper said, hands out in front of him as he approached her.

"I know," she said, her voice a whisper of sound.

"Viper!" It was the only warning Arkham could issue before the girl attacked. She launched herself at Viper. In reflex, he caught her.

Two things happened when he closed his arms around her. First, Viper recognized she was more than a girl. The woman had curves aplenty, two of which were mashed against his chest, rubbing over him with every movement of her body. Second, the woman was fucking *fierce*. Viper was perfectly capable of defending himself, but he was hesitant to do anything for fear of hurting her. So she pummeled him with that fucking rock. By sheer luck, she didn't catch his head with it, only his jaw. Viper retained his hold on her with one arm securely around her waist while using the other to block her blows as best he could. For such a small little thing, she packed quite a punch! Despite his efforts, she still connected several times before Arkham disarmed her. Bastard didn't help him any more than that. *And still, she fought.* Apparently frustrated with her lack of progress, Darcy shrieked, kicking out and continuing to hit at him with her fists.

"Knock it the fuck off, woman!" Viper finally set her on her feet and captured her wrists in his hands and wrapped his arms around her, trapping her with his superior strength. "Look at me, Darcy!" Viper used every ounce of command he possessed. In the end, it was probably the use of her name that made her pause in her tirade. "Look at me!" When she gave him a wary look he took a breath. "Your father sent us to find you and bring you home."

"I'm not going back! I'm old enough to make my own decisions, and I'll be damned if I go back to that bastard!" Her struggles resumed. She tried to hike her knee up into his groin, but he managed to avoid it, pulling her tighter against him. It was getting exceedingly hard to ignore the lush curves pressed against him. The woman was tempting in the worst way.

"You've never even met your dad," Viper said, struggling to hold her while not hurting her. "I assure you, he's a good man."

"Rayburn, my stepdad, is a molesting bastard and my mom is nothing more than his pimp! I'll kill both of them and you before I go back!"

Viper was so shocked, he relaxed his hold for a second, giving the girl enough leverage to break free. Darcy promptly kicked him in the balls before spinning around to flee again. Arkham caught her, spun her back around, and zip-tied her hands behind her back, ensuring he didn't get a repeat of what Viper got. Once she was secured, he looped a length of rope around her waist and tied her to a tree.

"That should take care of that." Arkham turned his attention to Viper, kneeling down beside his biker brother. "You gonna be all right?"

"Shut the fuck up, you smug bastard." Viper tried to sound menacing, but it was hard to do when his balls were stinging. Didn't help with him down on one knee looking up at the big man, either.

"Just trying to help a brother out." Arkham raised his hands in surrender before turning back to their prisoner.

"You gonna fight me, girl?"

"You gonna try to take me back to that hellhole?" She had to look up at Arkham, but Darcy didn't seem the least bit intimidated. In fact, she looked to be sizing him up, looking for the easiest way to take him down.

"Hadn't planned on it," he said.

When Arkham didn't offer anything else, Viper added, "It's your biological father who sent us. We're takin' you back to the clubhouse."

She looked from Arkham to Viper. "Biological father. Clubhouse?"

"Yeah." Viper groaned as he got to his feet. "Look. I'm Viper. This is Arkham. We've been huntin' you for three fuckin' days, sweetheart. I'd like to get out of the fuckin' snow."

"Three days? I've only been gone like five." They had Darcy's attention now. Viper could see her calming down and really listening to what they had to say.

"Data set us on you less than an hour after he got the news from your mother."

"Bullshit," she spat. "My mother hasn't had contact with my dad since right after I was born. She said he had no use for a kid."

"Don't know their story. Or yours." Viper shrugged. "All I know is a man as steady as a rock under any kind of pressure is on my ass in a big way to get you home and out of danger."

"Well, he hasn't been in my life for the first eighteen years. I don't need him for the next eighteen."

"You don't even want to hear what he has to say? Not gonna cost you anything but a few hours of your precious time. You don't like what he says or think he's feedin' you a line of bullshit, you can leave. Hell, I'll even take you anywhere you wanna go."

She was silent for a moment as she pondered what he'd said. Viper had to stifle a groan. It was the first time he'd had a chance to really study her. Her stocking hat had fallen free, releasing a riot of bright red curls that spilled around her face and down her back. Her skin was nearly as pale as the snow around her but smattered with a light dusting of freckles across her forehead and the bridge of her nose. Delicate eyebrows rose in a fiery arch above sparkling pale blue eyes. Her appearance matched her temper, but also gave a man black ideas. Like spreading her out right here in the snow and fucking her until they melted the clearing around them. God! Would she have fiery curls on her cunt? In an instant, Viper was hard and aching, his need to claim this woman here and now so strong he had to bite back a growl.

Finally she relaxed against her bonds. "Fine. Kinda cold out here anyways."

Viper started to release her, but Arkham stayed his hand, shaking his head.

"I said I'd go with you," she huffed. "Ain't that enough?"

Arkham raised an eyebrow at her. "Plan on keepin' my balls intact." He glanced at Viper. "He might not've learned his lesson, but I sure the fuck did."

Man had a point. Finally, Viper undid the rope, but left the zip tie around her wrists.

"Bastard," she muttered, but marched gamely between them.

"Got her," Viper notified Data. "It'll take us a while to hike out of here. Tell Trucker we'll meet him before dark."

"She OK?" Data sounded equal parts relieved and worried.

"Seems to be. I'll get a better assessment once we're out of here. Nothing I can do about it anyway if she is hurt. Not until we get to Trucker and the RV."

There was a pause before Data responded, "Keep me posted." That sounded more like the Data he was used to. Calm, cool, on top of things.

"Will do, brother."

It took the better part of three hours for them to make it back to the side-by-side they'd taken into the forest. Viper drove while Darcy sat passively beside him, never once complaining about the cold or the speed with which they traveled. They'd cut her bonds only to tie her again, this time with her hands in front of her for ease of travel. Arkham rode in the back bed of the vehicle.

Once they were out of the woods and on the little road leading out, Viper pushed them even faster. He felt the need to test the woman next to him. Would she tough it out or would she ask him to slow down? She hadn't said a word or in any way indicated she was uncomfortable, but her eyes squinted against the wind even though buffered by the windshield. She had on clothing appropriate for the weather so she couldn't be too bad off, but she hadn't had a chance to put her stocking hat back on and pull the mask down to cover her face. With her delicate white skin, she was rapidly picking up windburn, and all that fiery red hair whipped violently in the wind.

After ten minutes of riding, Arkham smacked the back of his head. Hard. Viper didn't have to ask to know what the other man meant. With a sigh, he let off the accelerator, slowing the vehicle to a more tolerable speed. A glance at Darcy revealed nothing of what she was thinking, her face a blank mask.

At the entrance to one of the many camping grounds inside the forest, they stopped. Trucker waited outside the RV the club owned. The man smiled warmly at Darcy as she climbed out of the side-by-side. Until he saw her wrists zip-tied together.

"What the fuck, Viper?" Immediately, Trucker whipped out his knife and started to undo her bindings. Arkham hastily grabbed his knife hand and pulled him back.

"Not a good idea, brother," the big man said. "Girl's feral."

Trucker glanced from Arkham to Viper. "You tell Data you're keeping his girl tied up?"

"No. And you're not either," Viper muttered. "Besides, once we're on the way I'll cut her loose."

Trucker sighed, scrubbing a hand through his shaggy beard. "Well, it's good to meet you, Darcy. Don't hold this against the rest of Bones. The rest of us are good people."

Arkham snorted.

Chapter Two

True to his word, Viper cut her bonds once they had her locked in the RV. She hated to admit it, but she was tired, cold, and damned hungry. They bounced around on the narrow road, but Viper still made her a sandwich. He handed her a Coke and a bag of chips to go with it and Darcy's mouth watered. She had to stop herself from cramming the stuff into her mouth like a starving child, instead forcing herself to eat one bite at a time. She had three bites of sandwich and a handful of chips gone before Viper opened a can of Beanie Weenies and stuck in a plastic spoon, sitting it in front of her along with another Coke. She glanced at him sharply but said nothing. Viper just shrugged. Apparently there was no hiding how hungry she was, so she gave up trying, gobbling the Beanie Weenies like they were the biggest, juiciest bone-in ribeye she'd ever dreamt about.

"Where'd you learn wilderness survival?" Viper sat back on the bench across from her, the table between them. The question was asked casually, but she could tell he was fishing for something.

"Mom was always sending me to camps. Summer. Winter. Didn't matter. When she was married to Calvin, they kept me gone as much as they could."

"Who's Calvin?"

"One of Mom's exes. They divorced when he figured out, accidentally you understand," she batted her eyelashes and looked as innocent as a newborn babe, "that Mom was steadily withdrawing money from his bank account. I think she managed to take nearly half his savings before he finally woke the fuck up and realized the Goddamned pussy just wasn't worth it."

When Viper nearly spewed his water, Darcy couldn't help but grin. "Little witch," he muttered. "So you learned survival at camp. This the first time you'd attempted in something other than an exercise?"

"Attempt? Bitch, I *did* it!" When Viper looked at her now-empty plate and raised an eyebrow, she rolled her eyes. "OK, so there are a few things I need to tweak, but I was five days alone in the wilderness and I'm still alive." She stuck her chin out stubbornly. This man was not going to belittle her skill. She might not be some kind of badass like he obviously was, but she'd broken free of an abusive situation and proven to herself she could survive on her own.

Surprisingly, he nodded. "You did." He jerked his chin to the back of the RV. "You want a hot shower, it's back there. Just don't take all day. Water's limited."

"Are you fucking kidding me? A shower? In a camper full of strange men? No thinks. I'll stink. Besides, I'm sure body odor inhibits rape. Maybe not much, but if that's on the agenda, I'm damned well gonna make sure you don't enjoy it." She was flippant about it, but Darcy couldn't help remember the pawing hands of her latest stepdad. The one time he'd caught her alone, he'd damned near completed the act. Too bad she'd taken all those self-defense classes her other stepdad had paid for at all those camps. That had been exactly two days before she'd split.

Arkham chuckled. "Look," he said, getting up from the passenger seat in the front and moving back to the table where she and Viper sat. "If you want to shower, I'll keep Viper here from jumping you." He raised his hands in a surrendering gesture. "You're too young for me, so I'll restrain myself."

"And you think I'll just believe you?"

"No. But the offer still stands." Viper shrugged. "Besides, you *do* stink. I'd think you'd want to meet your father not smelling like you'd been out in the wilderness by yourself for the better part of a week."

Darcy bared her teeth at him before turning her head to look out the window and ignore him. She just stifled the urge to sniff her pits. Bastard.

She rode for a long while in silence, not wanting to talk any of them. Partly because she was trying to be defiant. Partly because she knew they were right. She needed to take a shower or at least wash off.

Apparently the one called Viper had had enough. "Up with you, Lil' Bit." He stood, snagging her hand and tugging until he pulled her to her feet. "Time to stop being stubborn."

"I don't have any other clothes," she protested, dragging her feet as he led her toward the bathroom. "I can't take a shower only to put back on dirty clothes."

"I'll find you something. When we get to the clubhouse, the women will help out more." He opened the bathroom door and nudged her inside, not being rough but making his meaning clear. "Be quick about it." Then he shut the door, and she heard him moving about the RV.

What the hell had she gotten herself into? Despite her misgivings about being alone with three strange men, the shower called to her. They hadn't given her any reason to think she was in danger, so she sighed and stripped.

The shower warmed quickly, and the pressure was surprisingly strong. She found pleasantly scented shampoo and matching conditioner as well as shower gel sitting in a neat little row on the molded shelf and helped herself. God, the water felt heavenly! She hadn't realized how much she needed to be clean until she was scrubbing with her hands over her chilled skin as the water warmed her. Despite the situation, Darcy nearly sighed in contentment. She wished she had time to spend on her hair. Concentrating on the tangle inevitable in her curly hair helped center her. Unfortunately, she only had time to give herself a cursory wash. She'd just finished rinsing her hair and was about to turn the water off when the bathroom door opened.

"T-shirt, gym shorts, socks," Viper said. Darcy squealed and covered herself even though the frosted shower door blocked his view. "Ain't nothin' I ain't seen before," he muttered. "Also found you a hairbrush and toothbrush. Both still in the package. Figure the shorts are miles too big, but they got a drawstring to keep 'em from fallin' off. Shirt's too big, too, but you'll be covered and warm."

"'K." When she didn't hear the door close, she waited another minute before turning off the water. Darcy opened the shower door and peeked around it.

Viper stood there leaning against the vanity, arms crossed and a sexy, cocky grin on his face.

"What are you doing?" She squawked her outrage. "Get the fuck out!" Her heart pounded, and it wasn't all from fear. The man was... magnificent. Darcy wasn't normally attracted to the bad-boy type, but this guy...

OK, so there was nothing "boy" about Viper. He was all man. Bearded and tattooed, he was sexy and knew it. She doubted there was a woman within a hundred-mile radius who could resist him. Including her. Didn't mean she'd make it easy for him. He was exactly the type of man she didn't need in her life. She'd seen her mother bring home man after man just like him. All of them, without fail, had been bad news. Viper definitely fit that bill.

"Just makin' sure you were payin' attention."

"Why would you do that? What the fuck? Pervert!" Darcy poured all her outrage into her expletive, hoping like hell Viper didn't see through her. Because, no matter how much she wanted to deny it, she was seriously attracted to him. Being in the same room with him, naked as the day she was born, was a fucking turn-on, whether she intended to act on that attraction or not. Didn't mean her imagination wasn't running amok to hell and back.

"Never said I wasn't, Lil' Bit." He grinned as he straightened, then indicated the clothes he'd brought her. "We'll be at the clubhouse in about an hour. Expect you to be out of here and ready."

"Or what?" she asked defiantly. "You gonna beat my ass?"

"Might," he answered, a grin tugging wider at his full lips. "More likely, I'll just haul your pretty ass out, ready or not."

"Get out," she repeated.

With a chuckle, Viper pushed off the vanity and left, shutting the door behind him. Darcy stared after him for long moments, waiting to see if he'd come back in when he thought her guard was down. He didn't. Darcy quickly stepped out of the shower and wrapped a towel around her. He'd obviously picked the lock to get in, and she didn't trust any of them not to invade her privacy. A vision of all three of the big men holding her down and forcing themselves on her flashed through her mind, and she whimpered before she could stop the sound.

"You OK in there?"

Was Viper standing outside the door?

"Go away!" she yelled at him, not able to put as much force in her command as she'd have liked. She was shaken. Her stepfather had done that to her. Made fear her first reaction. Revulsion when these men were only trying to help. Was it ideal? No. This was exactly the sort of situation she should fear. Three strange men hunting her and picking her up out of the wilderness. No one knew where she was. Probably no one even cared. Yet, these guys had been kind. They'd fed and clothed her. Hadn't made any overt gestures to indicate she wasn't safe in their care. She was repaying them with suspicion and insults, none of which she could help. All because Rayburn had attacked her and shaken her belief in everyone around her. That, and the fact that her mother hadn't believed her, hadn't even contemplated she was telling the truth. Why should she believe a man she'd never met, a man claiming to be her biological father, would be any better?

Damn Rayburn! She'd hated him from the moment her mother had brought him home. He'd always leered at her, making her uncomfortable around him. When he'd attacked her, she hadn't been surprised. It did surprise her how the incident had colored her perception of men around her. Probably because she was stupid and naive.

She dressed quickly. No underwear, but the shirt came to her knees and the shorts halfway down her shins. Even if the drawstring failed, she would still be covered. Dressed, she brushed out her long hair, catching tangles for nearly ten minutes until she finally tamed the unruly curls. Once that was done, she sat on the toilet and put her head in her hands. She was so fucked.

A knock at the door made her cringe in frustration. "Can you not just leave me the fuck alone for five fucking minutes?"

Just as she'd suspected, the doorknob turned, and Viper stood in the opened doorway. He gave a heavy sigh before reaching his hand out to her. "Come on, Lil' Bit. Out with you."

"Fucker," she muttered but stood and let him lead her back to the table. She slid on the bench next to the window and watched the scenery pass as they drove toward their clubhouse and the man claiming to be her biological father.

"You know," she said, not looking at Viper, "I have no way of knowing if your friend is my father or not. I've never even seen a picture of him."

"Not sure it matters whether you're actually his or not. He's all in."

"Why would he do that? I mean, even if he was with my mom for any length of time, there's no telling if he actually fathered any child of hers. I say that with the knowledge of a daughter who has seen men come and go from her mother's bed all her life. My mom has no idea what the word fidelity means."

"All I know is he's frantic to get you to safety. Anxious to meet you. He's already claimed you as his so if he has doubts, he's not voicing them."

She turned to face Viper. "He doesn't have to. If he knows my mother at all, he knows the chances are just as high some other dumbass is my father."

For the first time, Viper's face turned hard. Even when she'd kneed him in the balls he hadn't seemed angry at her. Now she was afraid she might have pushed him just a little too far.

"Your father is many things, Darcy. But he's not a dumbass. He's probably the most intelligent man I've ever met. If he suspects anyone but him fathered you, he doesn't care. Your mother basically handed him a daughter, and he's grabbing hold with both hands."

"That makes no sense," she scoffed. "I'm a grown-ass woman. I don't need a daddy at this late date."

"Honey, every little girl needs a father figure. You might be all grown up, but you need to know there is always gonna to be one man in your life you can count on. Data's that man. Give him the chance to prove it."

"He gonna turn out to be some fucking pervert looking for someone to play into his daddy-porn fetish?" That got a growl from Viper, Arkham, and Trucker all three. Viper held her gaze, not saying anything. "What? It's a legitimate concern! You all may be Mother Teresa but how am I supposed to know that? You'll pardon me if I don't take your word for it." The man absolutely would *not* make her feel petty about this.

"No one's askin' you to take our word for it. Meet the man. Give him a chance. Know he sent out his brothers to find you when he couldn't."

"Couldn't?"

"We all have a set of skills. Your father is the intel guy. Nothing he can't do with a computer given enough time. No one he can't find."

"Except me before now." Darcy couldn't help the interruption. She wanted to be antagonistic. Needed to be if she was going to keep her composure.

"He had no reason to be trying because he didn't know you existed."

She could argue, but at this point there was really no reason for it. There was no way either of them could win. Instead, she turned back to the window and ignored Viper. It was what she did when she wanted people to leave her alone.

Thirty minutes later, they pulled into the driveway of what looked like a resort hotel or some shit. Nothing really fancy, but certainly not the roach-infested biker clubhouse she was expecting.

She also wasn't expecting the crowd pouring out of said clubhouse. There had to be thirty or forty men and women. All of them were wearing various pieces of leather, most motorcycle jackets or vests. When someone turned slightly, she saw the recognizable emblem of a motorcycle club with the name *Bones* above the emblem and the name of their city, Somerset, on the bottom. Some of the women had jackets or vests, but not many and, though dressed appropriately for winter, they wore clothing that accentuated their bodies, particularly their breasts. The men all looked rough, with tattoos and beards of varying lengths, but each one of them, to the man or woman, looked concerned. One man in particular was practically wringing his hands. The crowd surrounded him, some clapping hands on his shoulders in support. An older couple stood nearby, both offering their support and urging the obviously anxious man forward.

"Let's go, Lil' Bit." Viper grinned at her, extending his hand in an obvious command for her to take it. Naturally she wasn't going anywhere near that.

"Stop calling me that," Darcy snapped. "It's demeaning."

"Sure. Soon as you grow a foot and gain a couple hundred pounds."

She bared her teeth and hissed at him. Arkham came up behind Viper and smacked the back of his head, something the man obviously did often.

"Stop baiting her."

"But it's so much fun, and she rises to it so easily."

Darcy slid out of the seat and pushed around the two men to get to the exit. Too late, she realized her mistake. There had to be half a foot of snow outside, and she was standing there in her sock feet. Someone opened the door, and it was too late to back-pedal. Viper chuckled and lifted her into his arms. She was so startled not only did she squeal, but she wrapped her arms around his neck, clinging like a baby.

"That's my Lil' Bit," he praised next to her ear. "Now, let's go meet your family." She noticed he hadn't said "daddy" or "father." Apparently, Viper was smarter than she'd given him credit for. He understood her fears and respected them. Perhaps she needed to reassess this situation.

Chapter Three

"What the fuck happened to her?"

Viper winced at Data's cutting tone.

"You dunk her in water? It's fucking winter! What the fuck, Viper?"

"Dude, she took a shower," came Trucker behind them. "She was fine as frog hair when we found her. Little cold and hungry, but no worse for wear."

"Get her inside," Data ordered, ignoring the snickers around him. For such a mild-mannered man, he was turning into a regular overprotective biker dad.

"Relax, brother," Cain said, appearing from the crowd with his wife Angel in tow. "Angel and the women will get her comfortable, and we'll all sit down and have a chat."

"Cain, I didn't even know I had a fuckin' kid, much less a *daughter*! I can't relax!" He glanced at Viper, narrowing his eyes as the situation really sunk in. Without even realizing what he was doing, Viper settled her closer to him, knowing the other man was fixing to take his prize from him. Her arms sliding around his neck felt so fucking right. Like she'd been born to be in his arms. She was his. Destined. "Oh, no, Viper. No fuckin' way!"

Darcy looked from him to Data and back. "What?" Her arms tightened just that little bit around his neck and Viper's chest swelled. The feeling was uncomfortable, but not unpleasant.

Fuck.

Date stormed over to Viper, practically ripping Darcy from him. That feeling in his chest shattered, nearly bringing Viper to his knees. "Fucker," he muttered, taking a breath to clear his head as he followed Data and everyone else inside. Arkham clapped a hand on his shoulder.

"Pussy whipped without gettin' the pussy is pretty fuckin' sad, Viper."

"Have you always been such an insufferable bastard?"

Arkham shrugged. "Never thought about it."

"Well think on it. One of these days, your turn's comin'."

"Not bloody likely."

Once inside, the ol' ladies surrounded Darcy, hugging her and welcoming her to the family. Viper was gratified to see her glancing his way more than once. Always he nodded to her encouragingly, hoping she'd find her footing easily. He stayed close, though, unable to let her out of his sight.

"What's goin' on between the two of you?" Cain had sidled up to Viper, handing him a beer.

Viper took a long pull, thinking about his answer. *What, indeed*? "Honestly? Nothin'. She's distrustful of me, and I'm too old for her."

"Damned straight," Data interjected as he joined them. "Way too fuckin' old." The man took a pull of his own beer. He turned his head and met Viper's gaze. "You've had my back more than once in the field, Viper. You're my brother. Don't make me have to kill you."

Cain chuckled. Viper grinned, though he couldn't put his heart into it. Mainly because he was very afraid he'd end up fighting Data one day. Not exactly a fair fight since Data was the geek. Sure, he was wiry and muscled, deadly as any of them, but Viper was definitely the stronger of the two.

"Before you go thinkin' you can take me, Viper, remember I'm smarter'n you."

"No question there," Viper agreed. "Never said you weren't. Never said we were gonna fight, either."

"Didn't have to. I saw the way you held Darcy. The way you're lookin' at her now." Data gave him a look that was positively chilling. "She might be a tough girl, but she ain't ready for a man like you."

"Noted," Viper acknowledged. Had he put it any other way, Viper might have shrugged him off and done whatever the hell he wanted to. But Data was right. Viper didn't know much about Darcy, but he knew by the glimpses she'd given him into her relationship with her mother and stepfather the girl wasn't nearly ready for a man like him. Not only was he at least fifteen years her senior, but he was a seasoned, jaded man sexually. No way she'd welcome his advances.

"You know much about her current stepdad?" This had to be dealt with. If Data didn't want to get involved with it, considering his ex might be personally responsible for anything that had happened to Darcy, Viper would damned well make it his own priority.

"No, but I've been looking into him. Once I knew you had Darcy I was able to get a fuckin' grip." He glanced at Cain when the man snorted. "OK, so maybe I don't exactly have a grip on any fucking thing right now. But I did look into Donna's life after we parted ways."

"Thought you guys kept in touch after you split?" Viper took another pull of his beer, his gaze straying back to Darcy and the other women.

"We did. Bitch didn't tell me we had a kid, and I didn't pry into her personal life. To tell the truth, I was glad she was gone. She stayed in touch because occasionally she needed something and knew I was the man who could get it for her. No matter what it was."

"Did you?" Viper couldn't help ask the question.

"Of course I did." Data shrugged. "No reason not to."

"Darcy says she's had it rough."

Data's focus was instantly on Viper, full and terrible. "What do you mean 'rough?'"

"Says her mother's current husband was... inappropriate."

There was a hard silence while Data stared at him, seething. "Define... 'inappropriate.'"

"Didn't go into it. But she called him a molesting bastard. Said her mother was nothing more than his pimp. Her exact words. Not paraphrased."

Data closed his eyes, his jaw tightening almost convulsively. "Imma beat the shit outta those motherfuckers. Right before I kill 'em."

"Just calm down," Cain said. "I hear ya, Data, and Bones will help. But you ain't goin' into this shit halfcocked. This is just like anything else we do. We'll investigate, plan, then execute."

"You gonna let her mother know you found her?" Viper took the last three swallows of his beer and set the bottle down. A club girl was there to take it and hand him a fresh one. "Has she been asking?"

"No," Data said immediately. "And no. It was a long time ago we were together, but she's every bit as self-centered as I remember her being." He looked over to the women, his troubled gaze landing on Darcy. "She looks so much like my sister it's scary," he muttered.

Viper chose to let Data keep his musings to himself, figuring it was a private observation. He cleared his throat. "Then a total blackout of information. Does she know where to find you?"

"Not sure. Donna and I were together when I was still prospecting for Bones. Right when I'd left the service and had just started working for ExFil. A couple years after the rest of you started Bones."

"I remember," Cain said, sitting up straighter at the bar. "She was that little blonde with the big tits."

"You remember every woman by the size of their tits?" Data sounded a cross between exasperated and amused.

Cain shrugged. "Not saying I don't. But if you tell Angel, I'll swear you lied."

Viper snorted. Data saluted him with his beer bottle.

"So, what do we do now?" Viper had a vested interested in Data's plans for Darcy. He intended on getting to know the curvy little redhead better, whether or not Data wanted him to.

"Nothing," Data said. "Keep her safe and inside as much as possible. She's legal. She can do what she pleases, but I'm not invitin' trouble."

"Let the women get her involved in decoratin' for Christmas," Cain said, a satisfied grin on his face. "Didn't realize how much this place would liven up when they got to doing shit like that. Angel's wantin' to get together a group of us to go to the hospital and give out presents."

"I knew they had something planned," Data groaned. "What is it with women and Christmas?"

Viper shrugged. "Dunno. But I appreciate those little Santa nighties they always seem to come up with. Little poofy white shit hugging their tits…" He grinned wickedly. "Oh yeah."

"You're such a pervert." Cain laughed. "But you're right." He glanced at his wife, who had her head back, laughing with Luna and Magenta. Darcy had a grin on her face, reserved but receptive. "Think I need to collect my wife for a bit."

"She doin' OK?"

"Yep. Has morning sickness every morning at exactly six, but otherwise doesn't seem to have any problems at all now."

"You and Bohannon are lucky men," Viper admitted. For the first time, he wondered what it would be like to be expecting a child of his own. Which made him think about Data. How would he feel if a man older than he was wanted to date his daughter? Viper knew the answer to that question. He'd beat the fuck out of the other man and ask forgiveness of his daughter later.

Cain clapped Viper on the shoulder. "Think before you do anything stupid, brother," he muttered as he left the bar and sidled up to his ol' lady. Angel was practically glowing with her pregnancy. When Cain wrapped his arms around her, caressing her baby bump, Viper didn't know whether to sigh or vomit.

"Do all men turn into pussies when they get a woman?"

Data snorted. "I did. Until I realized what a fucking bitch she was." He gripped Viper's arm. "You remember that. I'm sure you don't want to be a pussy. Right?"

"You warning me off?"

"You know it, brother." There was no humor in his expression.

* * *

Darcy had been so wrapped up in her own problems that she'd nearly forgotten Christmas was in three weeks. The weather hinted at a white Christmas, and she would normally be excited as shit. Now?

Meh.

She'd never felt welcome after her mother had married fucking Rayburn. The last two Christmases had been less than celebratory. His daughters -- who were both older than she was -- were perfect. She was confrontational, something both Rayburn and her mother had pointed out to her daily. Darcy hadn't been a biddable addition to the family, and she had no desire to be added to Rayburn's harem. As far as she knew, there was no incest or anything going on with his biological daughters, but the man fucked anything else with a pussy. He was, in a word, *disgusting*.

"Hey, Darcy," Angel called, leaning back against Cain, her husband. The man had his arms around her, his hands covering her tummy and the obvious baby bump. "Can you take over light duty for me? Cain has a little something I need to inspect for him." She giggled when the man growled and bit her neck.

"Little? I'll show you little." When he scooped her up and strode out of the great room, Angel laughed merrily. Darcy couldn't help but envy her.

"You heard her, Darcy." Luna shoved her a bundle of tangled lights nearly as big as she was. "Light duty."

"That's not fair," Magenta chastised Luna, giggling the entire time. "Don't give the new girl a chore like that. She'll run away from us screaming."

"Yeah," Luna said, rubbing her lip thoughtfully. "But those things never turn out so well. I can attest to it. The men just drag you back caveman style." She gave a heavy sigh. "It's a good thing they make up for it in other ways."

Both women continued to laugh merrily. Another woman across the room handed Arkham and Trucker beer before going to the stereo and turning on a cheerful round of Christmas music.

"Jesus, woman," a guy hollered from across the room, sounding put out as hell. "Do you have to play that racket all the damned time? This is a clubhouse, not a *cunt* house."

Everyone laughed.

As she stood there, trying like hell to be a part of the women's circle, Darcy felt more and more out of place. Uncomfortable. Every single one of them was happy, laughing and joking with each other. Even the men joined in despite each of the three women being with one of their brothers. No one crossed a line, or acted inappropriate; rather they seemed like siblings in a big house. It made Darcy long for that camaraderie. That… acceptance.

She looked around the room until her gaze collided with Viper's. He was drinking a beer at the bar, leaning lazily against the polished wood. He nodded at her once before turning his attention back to the buxom woman standing next to him. Irrationally, Darcy felt a spike of jealousy. Viper might be crass and fucking annoying, but he was hers, Goddamnit! At least, that's the way it felt. Why, she had no idea. She didn't even like the bastard. But when he called her Lil' Bit, her heart squeezed and her insides turned to mush. He'd same as staked a claim but only to her. Made her want to scratch his eyes out to watch him smile at the woman standing next to him.

With a defiant raise of her chin, Darcy firmly turned away from him and continued with her task of untangling the lights. The women chattered lightly while lively Christmas music played around them. In the big hearth across the room a fire roared, creating a cozy atmosphere, especially with all the garland and other decorations going up.

She was about to give in to the temptation of looking at Viper again when Data, the man convinced he was her father, approached her.

"They being nice to you?" He indicated the other women engaged in various tasks.

"Yeah." She gestured to the bundle of lights she was untangling. "Could be worse, I guess."

"You know, you don't have to fu -- er, mess with that shi -- uh stuff if you don't want to." The urge to giggle was just too strong. Darcy ducked her head, not wanting to hurt his feelings, but him trying to stifle his language in front of her was just too much. "I was just tryin' to be responsible," he grumbled. But she saw the smile tugging at his lips.

"I'm an adult, you know. And I swear just as much as any of you, I'm sure."

"Yeah, but a dad shouldn't curse in front of his daughter."

They were silent for a long while. Data even helped her pull at the tangled wires in her lap. It wasn't awkward, rather companionable. One question burned in Darcy though.

"Why are you convinced I'm your daughter? Mom was never faithful to anyone. I could be anyone's."

Data looked at her a long time, his gaze hard and penetrating. She was about to apologize for questioning him when he took out his wallet and pulled out a picture. Handing it to her he said, "Gloria. My younger sister. She died from cancer when she was about your age." The picture was worn, tattered around the edges and obviously at least a decade old, but the woman in the picture could have been Darcy's twin.

"Wow," she said. "I guess that's where I get my red hair from."

"And your personality. Viper and Arkham told me about them finding you and you fighting them. Did those assholes hurt you?"

"No. I'm good. I think I hurt Viper worse than he did me."

"Oh?"

"I thought you said he told you about me putting up a fight?"

"They did. Just said they had to restrain you."

Darcy grinned. "I got Viper in the balls. Dropped him to his knees. Would have gotten away except Arkham caught me. He's the one who tied me up."

Data looked at her like she'd grown two heads. "You... got Viper in the... balls?"

"Yeah."

It was long moments before Data started to chuckle. Then laugh. Then guffaw until tears were rolling down his cheeks. There was no way to keep from joining his merriment.

They were still laughing when a girl of about eleven or twelve joined them. "Need some help?"

"Yeah," Darcy said. "We could use some."

"My name's Suzie. What's yours?"

"This is my daughter, Darcy," Data said, his chest puffing out just a little. That little show of pride made Darcy's heart ache. No one had ever introduced her as their anything, yet here this stranger was, willing to claim her as his family. "She's going to be with us a while. Darcy," he turned to her, "this is

Suzie. Girl's sharp as a tack. She has two foster brothers around here somewhere."

"Cliff and Daniel," she supplied. "But they're stinky and nobody likes them." The mischievous grin said she didn't really think so but liked teasing them.

"We heard that, you little imp!" The admonishment came from across the room. Two young men were dutifully hanging up garland but stopped to glare at the girl. Neither of them looked really put out. Suzie just giggled.

"I'll leave you two at the lights," Data said. "I have a couple of things to finish and it could take a couple of hours." He looked at Darcy before getting up. "You need anything, you come find me. Anything at all, you understand?"

"Thanks," she said. Maybe he wasn't all that bad.

"Oh," he said as he got to his feet. "And one other thing." She looked at him questioningly. "Viper is a player. Might be best if you steer clear of him."

She tilted her head. "You warning me off because you don't like him?"

He shrugged. "More because I don't want to have to kill my brother when you get hurt."

"Why would you do that?" It was a legitimate question. No one had ever come to her defense before. Especially not over something like this.

"Because you're my daughter. I might not have been in your life, but I swear it wasn't because I didn't want to be. I protect my family. With my life." With that, he turned and walked away.

"Pretty neat, huh?" Suzie whispered. "They're all like that. They follow through, too. When me and Cliff and Daniel and Angel were in trouble, they had to kill a few people after they attacked the club." She scrunched her nose, but talked about the carnage matter-of-factly. "They protected us. Now, once the guys are old enough, they're gonna let them prospect for Bones. If they prove themselves, they'll be patched members. Maybe even get to work in Cain's army."

Darcy blinked. "Cain has an army?"

"Yeah. They go on missions and everything. It's all really cool."

"Well, OK then." Darcy had no idea what to make of that.

"Ask Viper about it. He'll explain."

"Are you going to be in Cain's army, too?"

"I hope so. Only I'll do stuff like Data does. He says I've got the mind for it. He works with the computers and stuff. I'm learning. It's really fun." She grinned from ear to ear.

"Data a good guy?" Figured she might as well troll for information if she could. She'd need it if she intended to stay here any length of time.

"Oh, yeah. All of them are, though they try to pretend they're all bad and stuff. Underneath, they're really all just teddy bears."

A collective groan rose around them. Obviously, their conversation wasn't at all private.

"Ah, come on, Suzie!"

"I ain't no fuckin' teddy bear. Kid's lying!"

"Cain! Come do somethin' with that girl. She's tellin' tales again!"

The women all laughed. It was then she noticed Viper coming in her direction. He had a beer bottle in each hand. He handed her one. "Can I borrow Darcy for a while, Suzie?"

The girl looked from one to the other. "Sure." She grinned. "I think he likes you," she whispered as she stood with the ball of lights and headed in the direction of her foster brothers.

Chapter Four

Darcy took the beer he handed her, took a pull, then grimaced. Girl didn't like beer so well. "Got some clothes for you. Women got together before we got here and bought you some stuff. Angel wanted everything but the underwear washed before you put it on, even though it was all brand new. Something about the dyes being bad for delicate skin. Said the underwear was different because it was... I don't know," he searched for the right phrasing when he didn't understand it himself.

"Because it's underwear?" Darcy grinned. "She's right about that. I have to get underwear out of a pack before I wear it. Anything else is just gross." The woman had such a beautiful smile that revealed the most intriguing dimples.

"Yeah," he said, answering her grin with one of his own. "When I think of it that way, I guess I understand what they meant." He cleared his throat. Was he actually *nervous* around a woman? What the fuck? "There's also toiletries and other things for you. Got 'em in your room."

She blinked. "I have a room?"

He wanted to answer, "Yeah. Same as my room," as he dragged her to his room but refrained. On both counts. "Thought I'd show you and give you the grand tour." He held out a hand to her. She looked hesitant but took his hand anyway. Probably an automatic reaction on her part. Didn't matter. Viper didn't relinquish her hand.

"I would definitely like to change," she admitted. "And take a good shower. I still feel a bit grimy."

"I was kidding, you know." Viper knew he was acting completely out of character, but he seemed unable to get it together.

"About?"

"You didn't stink."

There was a silence before she ducked her head and giggled. "You're so full of shit."

"Come on," he growled as he pulled her deeper into the clubhouse. "Club officers have rooms on the top level. Club girls who stay here are on the second floor. Everyone else is on the ground floor." He kept her hand as he took her up the stairs and about halfway down the hall. Then Viper handed her a key and nodded to the door. "You'll stay here until you and Data work something out. Like all the other women, Mama and Pops, and the kids, being on the middle floor puts you between the club members. Offers a double layer of protection."

"Protection? I need protection?"

Viper shrugged. "This is an active MC. What we do is mostly legal, but we've made enemies over the years. Currently, there's a club in Nashville and one in Lake Worth, Florida, we're keepin' an eye on. Don't think they're an active threat. More like enemies watchin' each other. But we don't take chances with our women."

That little tidbit of information raised Darcy's eyebrows. "Almost seems like you're using it as an excuse to make sure your women don't leave without permission." She opened the door and stepped inside. Viper followed right on her heels. It made her uncomfortable, but not necessarily in a bad way. Darcy liked the heat of him at her back.

"Won't deny we like knowin' who's here and who's gone, but it really is for protection. Club was attacked a few months ago. Anyone livin' here, we protect. Keepin' the women and children between us is the best way to do that."

He shut the door and pulled her to him, all Data's warnings and his own good intentions going out the door the second she was mashed against him. Kissing her was imperative. And, sweet Jesus, she was *delicious*!

Viper swept his tongue inside at her first gasp, taking what he needed before she pushed him away. Or slapped him. He wasn't sure which he was hoping for because the fiery temper she showed on occasion turned him on something fierce. To his surprise -- and delight -- she did neither. Her hands landed on his shoulders lightly, and she was completely still for several moments as if stunned. Then she moaned, melting against him, meeting his kisses with some of her own.

There was no containing his growl as Viper continued to kiss her. Darcy clung sweetly to him, her little nails digging into his shoulders, holding him to her. He was playing a dangerous game. It wasn't Data, but Darcy he was worried about. She might be a capable, tough woman, but Data was right. She couldn't handle him. Data knew it, even if he didn't yet know his daughter. Hell, what man would want his daughter involved with a man like Viper? He'd been a Marine. Force Recon. He'd been dropped in the most dangerous of situations, done what he had to do, then disappeared without a trace. He wasn't a kind and gentle man. Viper was the Devil himself when he needed to be. And he always had his brothers' backs. Even at the expense of his own family. Hell, Bones, his biker brothers, *were* his family. At least, the only family who mattered. How could he explain that to Darcy?

How could he explain it to Data? His brother was right. She deserved better than him.

He ended the kiss as quickly as he'd started it, pushing her away from him like *she* should have done in the first damned place. First thing he intended to make sure Data taught Darcy was self-preservation.

"There," he said flippantly. "Been wantin' to do that since you got me in the privates." He grinned at her, trying to pull himself away from her emotionally when everything inside him was screaming for him to make her his. "Consider that a lesson in what happens when you fuck with badass bikers."

The second he uttered the words, Viper regretted them. Darcy's face went from beautifully dazed with lust to confused to hurt in the space of about three seconds. Then she just shut down.

"Well. Lesson learned, I guess. Now, if you'll excuse me, I'd like to change into something more fitting the weather." She crossed to the door and opened it again, leaving no doubt she wanted him gone. It was no more than he deserved. He'd acted on his needs, then tried to backtrack the only way he could, and Darcy had paid the price.

"Darcy…"

"Now, please," she said, forestalling anything he might have said by way of apology.

"See you around."

"No. You won't."

She firmly shut the door in his face, the lock clicking solidly.

"Fuck," he muttered as he stomped back to the stairs. He'd dug his own hole here. But maybe it was for the best. If Data knew he'd kissed her, he'd likely try to castrate Viper. If their positions were reversed, Viper would certainly beat the fuck outta Data.

Oh, well. What was done was done. Now, he had to help his brother with whatever Data needed to do by way of dealing with Darcy's mother and stepfather. That man had a beating coming. If not an early grave.

* * *

The second she had the door locked, Darcy dissolved into tears, sliding down the door into a heap on the floor. The whole week finally caught up with her. Not only did her own mother not want her, but she'd just been made a fool in front of a man like Viper. He was obviously used to casual hook-ups. Though she'd had plenty of sex since losing her virginity at seventeen, she'd only had one lover. They'd explored sex at length, experimenting with all kinds of things from straight fucking to light BDSM. Nothing too heavy and always with pleasurable results. But nothing in her experience had prepared her for that single kiss from Viper.

Dragging in a deep breath as she tried to dry her tears, Darcy headed for the bed where the women had left the clothing they'd bought for her in a neat stack. They were still warm from the dryer. She chose a pair of jeans and a soft sweater, and a matching sports bra and panties set before stepping into the shower.

Twenty minutes later she stepped out and then started brushing her long red hair. Though there was still a lingering feeling of being sorry for herself, the worst of her crazy emotions had settled. The thick mass of curls seemed to be a perpetual rat's nest, but she was ruthless when detangling it. Just one more soothing ritual to center her. Until the brush ran through unhindered, she kept at it. It took another twenty minutes with the hair dryer she'd been thoughtfully provided with before her hair was dry enough for her to dress without getting the back of her sweater damp where her hair would hang heavily. Normally, the ritual of fussing with her hair relaxed her. Centered her when she needed it to. Now, it just exhausted her. If it hadn't been early afternoon, she'd have just said fuck it and gone to bed. Instead, she got dressed, resigned to make the best of the situation.

The jeans were soft and flexible. The sweater was deep emerald cashmere that molded to her breasts and hugged her waist before settling over her hips lovingly. Even without makeup, she was passable. Where the women had gotten such fine garments she had no idea, because she absolutely would not believe they'd picked them up at Goodwill or Wal-Mart. They most certainly had not washed that damned sweater, but there was a dry-cleaning tag on it. How they'd gotten stuff like this so quickly she had no idea, but she would make sure to thank them.

Slipping on socks and shoes -- also new -- she ventured outside her room, down the stairs, and back to the common room where Christmas was in full swing. Had she not been so apprehensive about running into Viper, she would have smiled. The two teenage boys were busy decorating the tree under Suzie's direction. The girl was like a general, giving specific instructions and correcting the boys' mistakes quickly. The boys scowled at her until they turned their backs on her and flashed each other a grin. Obviously there were dynamics there.

One big, burly biker sat at the table where Suzie was decorating his beard with green and red glitter. The guy looked disgruntled but resigned to his fate. One look at him and he narrowed his eyes, daring her to giggle. Not that she or anyone else was going to, given that look on his face. It said something like, *"I will fucking take you down. Hard.*" Instead, Darcy gave him a two-finger salute and continued into the common room.

The first thing she saw when she rounded the corner fully into the common area was Viper sitting at the bar across the room, a woman standing between his legs with her hands on his shoulders, her head thrown back, laughing merrily. He wasn't actually touching her, but pain sliced through Darcy's heart for no reason other than her own stupidity. Data had warned her, yet she'd allowed him to kiss her. Had kissed him back instead of taking another shot at his privates. He might be a jackass, but her feelings were nobody's fault but her own.

Instead of lingering, she went straight to the tree the kids were working on. "Need some help?"

Suzie gave an exasperated huff, throwing her hands in the air. "These blockheads can't do anything right." She pointed to a particular ornament. It looked the same as all the other sparkling balls to Darcy, but what did she know? "You see that? Why did they put it *there*? Anyone can see it needs to go over here!" She pointed to a spot just out of her reach. Daniel sighed and moved the glittering ornament where she indicated. "Are you going to leave it hanging lopsided? Really, Daniel. You have no sense of style."

Cliff gave a barking laugh before covering it with a cough. Several of the men in the room hooted. The big guy sitting at the table with glitter in his beard merely grunted, still looking supremely pissed off, but taking it.

"How horrible," Darcy said, hiding her own grin.

"I know, right?" The girl placed her hands on her hips. "Men have no taste."

"Can't argue with that," Luna called from across the room. "This one was having a fit about the lights I strung up on the balcony."

"That's cause it's like a fuckin' spotlight shining directly into the room, blinkin' furiously," Bohannon groused. "Honestly, woman. You're gonna make me have a seizure one night."

"See? Show me a man who appreciates Christmas lights, and I might faint from the shock."

All the women laughed. The men just grunted or growled. Suzie giggled as she got Cliff, this time, to move another ornament. "Hey, Daniel," Cain called from where he was cuddling his wife on the love seat in front of the tree. "Isn't that the same ornament she just had you move?"

Daniel looked over his shoulder at the tree, his eyes narrowing. "Yeah. It is." He stood, moving closer to the tree for a better look. "And she had him put it in the same damned spot it was in before I moved it! You little terror!" Suzie squealed and ran, dodging both Cliff and Daniel deftly, as if she'd done so a thousand times before. Just when Darcy was sure they'd catch the girl and make good on their threat to tickle her until she farted, she jumped into the arms of the big guy with the glitter beard.

Both boys immediately skidded to a halt. The big man stood with Suzie in his arms, protecting her from the threat of her foster brothers. He looked as menacing as anything Darcy had ever seen.

"Easy there, Stunner," Daniel said, his hands out as if he were talking down a terrorist or something. "We were just playing."

"Besides," Cliff said, picking up where Daniel left off, "she's got it coming. You saw what she was doing."

The big man just growled and bared his teeth.

"OK, then." Daniel backed away slowly, not making any sudden moves. Like Stunner was a big ole grizzly bear ready to spring at any second. "We'll just be over here. You know. Rearranging all the ornaments on the tree."

Stunner growled again, louder this time.

"Or not," Cliff muttered. Both boys shuffled away.

Neither touched the Christmas tree. Suzie just giggled and wrapped her skinny arms around Stunner.

"You know I love you best, right?" Her voice was almost a whisper, but not quite. The big man puffed out his chest, but didn't say a word.

Darcy grinned at the girl when Stunner set her down and resumed his silent vigil while she painted snowflakes on his cheeks above his beard. He was stoic about it.

"Wow," Darcy said. "You've got one hell of a bodyguard there."

"Yep." She flashed Stunner a brilliant smile. "Stunner is my very own bad biker." She leaned forward to Darcy, adding in a true whisper, "I'm not supposed to say badass."

"Gotcha," Darcy said in the same whisper.

She looked up at Stunner. "You seen Data? I thought I'd spend some time with him." If she stayed much longer, she was going to look at Viper and his biker chick at the bar again. If she saw them kissing, she knew she'd vomit right there. Suzie would definitely not appreciate it if she did.

He jerked his head sideways. "Control room." His voice was deep and gruff, like he didn't often speak.

"Thanks." She looked at Suzie. "You keep those boys in line. Make sure they do right by that tree."

"You got it!" She saluted Darcy smartly, then continued painting Stunner's face. The girl seemed young for her age, though everyone spoke to how brilliant she was. She seemed almost childlike in her mannerisms. While she'd been getting to know the other women, they'd told her little Suzie was a holy terror at the computer. She was absorbing everything Data could teach her and learning a few tricks on her own. At the same time, she played like a little kid. Hence the glitter currently all over Stunner's beard. Why the big man allowed it was something she'd have to ask about in order to satisfy her own curiosity.

She turned in the direction Stunner had indicated and down a wide hallway. Music was blaring from the open door of an office. Data, supposedly her father, sat behind the desk, his feet propped up, air drumming to the beat as numbers flew by on the big monitor faster than she could keep up with.

"Hey," she said. Data nearly turned the chair over backward in his haste to get his feet down.

"Hey yourself. Have a seat."

"Whatcha doing?"

He grinned at her. "Nothing interesting."

"Uh huh. I get that same look and give that same answer when I'm doing something that could get me in trouble but am having too good a time to worry about getting caught."

Data snorted and gave her a lopsided smile that faded. Then he sighed. "I'm tracking down your mother."

Instantly, her good humor vanished. "I ain't goin' back to her, Data. I'll leave here and disappear before I do that."

"Relax, baby. No one is going to make you go anywhere. You're old enough to do whatever you want so your wishes are all I need to hear to make it happen. However, your mother has a lot to answer for. So does your stepfather."

"What are you going to do to them?"

"How much do you really care, Darcy?" he said, his entire demeanor changed in an instant. Gone was the easygoing man he'd shown her thus far. In his place was a dangerous predator. This was a man she wouldn't want to fuck with. "Be careful before you answer. Because I will tell you whatever you want to know, but your wishes won't change my decisions. She'll get to give her say, but there is nothing that can excuse what she allowed to happen to you."

She did as he asked. She considered everything. This was a man who was going to punish the people who'd harmed his daughter. In this, she could see Data wasn't a forgiving man. Did she really want to know? Yes, she decided. She did. But not right now. "I want to be there when you question her and her sack-of-shit husband. I think I have a right."

"Will you tell me exactly what happened? I need to know, not only about Rayburn Mills, but Donna as well. I need you to lay it out there, no matter how painful."

She shrugged. "Doesn't matter. It's still my word against theirs. Do what you need to do."

Data winced. Darcy wished she could give him what he wanted, but just thinking about it made her skin craw and an evil slime fill her veins. It was just too disgusting to relive this soon.

"It matters, Darcy. If you don't feel comfortable talking to me, perhaps Cain would give permission for you to talk to his wife and let her relay your story."

She thought about it for a few moments, looking at the suggestion from every angle. There was a very real possibility Data intended to punish both her mother and Rayburn. Severely. Did she want to let another person tell her story?

"No. If it comes to it, I'll tell you everything. But I'll do it in front of my mother and her husband. If I have to retell it, I want them both to have to sit through it and hear me tell it in front of everyone. Just like if we were in a real court of law. That's the only fair thing to do."

Data raised his chin. "You're a remarkable woman, Darcy," he said in a reverent tone. "If nothing else, you've earned my respect for this alone."

The admission shocked Darcy. In her life, she could never remember anyone giving her praise for anything. For this, Data, and Bones by extension, deserved her to give them a chance. A wholehearted chance.

"Data," she said, reluctant to bring up the subject, but compelled to do so. "Why did you send Viper after me?"

Again, her father's demeanor changed. Again, he looked dangerous as hell. "I sent Viper, Arkham, and Trucker after you. Why would you single out Viper?"

She winced. "Caught that, did you?"

"Darcy…"

"Look, you've asked some hard things of me here. I'll do what I have to because if those two will prey on me, I'm certain they'll prey on other women who can't defend themselves as well as I can. So, I'm acknowledging this is hard for you, too."

He sighed. "Fair enough. What do you want to know?"

"You said he's a player."

"I did."

She swallowed, not sure how to voice what she needed. "He... kissed me. Earlier today." When Data's face turned thunderous, she quickly added, "Don't get all papa bear on me. I kissed him back just as hard. What I'm asking is, did he know you objected to him hooking up with me?"

"Oh, that asshole knew perfectly well I didn't want him near you like that."

"Then why would he do it?" She hated that she sounded a little like a child who'd just gotten her heart broken, but she actually felt a little like it. "He said it was in retaliation for me kicking him in the balls, but..."

"You think he did it deliberately to go against me? Darcy, he's my brother in every way that matters. If he made a move on you knowing I didn't want him to, there was a reason for it."

"Like what?"

"Not sure," Data muttered, but he stood, towering over Darcy. He framed her face with his big hands, leaning in to brush a kiss on top of her head. "But I'll find out."

Chapter Five

Viper frowned at the monitor in front of him. Since he couldn't take Darcy to his room and explore her at his leisure, he'd decided to throw all his effort into finding her mom and stepfather. Data might be the information and communication master of the club, but Viper had learned a thing or two during his time in Force Recon. One thing was for sure. The couple hadn't gone to California like they'd told Data. He'd found them and their two older daughters in Vegas. Sure seemed like they hadn't worried over much over their missing family member enough to even give Data a reliable means of contacting them when he found her. Apparently, "done" really meant done.

"When this is over," Data said, coming up behind him, "I'm gonna beat your fuckin' ass from here to China."

Viper winced. "She told you, didn't she?"

"I told you to fuckin' leave her alone, you bastard. Why did you just have to go against me? You've got any woman you want right here. Why didn't you just leave my daughter alone like I asked you?"

Data slammed the door behind him, and Viper knew they were about to have it out right here. He also knew he wouldn't lift a finger to do more than defend himself. If that. Any beating Data dished out, Viper knew he deserved.

"There's nothing I can say to explain that, Data. I'm not sure I understand it myself, but I know I can't promise I won't do it again."

Viper expected the other man to charge him. A fistfight was on point with the situation. Instead, Data pulled out his sidearm, cocked it, and pointed it right between Viper's eyes.

"Give me one good reason I shouldn't blow your fuckin' head off." This was a side of Data Viper had never seen. There was no doubt the man truly wanted to kill Viper for what he saw as disrespect to Darcy and a blatant disregard for his wishes regarding her. "Just because she's one of us doesn't mean she's fair game for any patched member here. She's my daughter, whether or not I've been in her life until now. So I'm asking you now. Man to man. What are your intentions toward my daughter?"

The situation was surreal. The question cliché. What exactly *were* his intentions with Darcy? "She's..." He struggled to find the right word.

"Think hard about your next words, Viper," Data said, taking a step closer so the barrel of his pistol rested against Viper's forehead. "I *will* hold you accountable for them."

"Data, Darcy is..." He shook his head, not believing what he was about to blurt out. "She's mine." He held up a hand in warning, knowing by the look on Data's face he wasn't intimidated by Viper. "Before you go jumping to conclusions, let me tell you I just realized it when you made me choose. I want her. Not necessarily for the reasons you're thinking, either." He cocked his head, then shook it. "OK, so maybe for the reasons you're thinking, but not as a hookup or temporary affair." He took a breath then sagged as if defeated. "I want her for my own. She's the one, Data. Mine."

It seemed like an eternity before Data lowered his weapon. He still didn't holster the thing, or even speak. Not for a very long time.

"Say something, brother."

"If you break her heart, Viper, I swear, I'll kill you. Slowly. Then I'll get Mama and Pops to revive you so I can do it again."

"She got under my skin, man. I can't explain it even to myself. She's blunt to the point of being a brat, just as crass as I am, and utterly indomitable when she decides she's set her mind to something. I saw that during the last three days I tracked her and during the ride home. I'm going to get to know her better and be what she needs."

"Why?" Data demanded.

"Fuck if I know," Viper muttered. "Because I *have* to."

"She's confused about you already. You think long and hard before you do anything else. I told her you're a player. I'm not backing down from that stance, but I won't hinder you, because she's an adult. I'll answer her questions about you honestly, but she will make her own decisions without my interference." He took another step toward Viper. Now, Data stood nose to nose with him. The size difference in the two was so different Viper would have laughed under any other circumstances. Now, he could actually feel the animosity directed at him from his brother. This might be the one time in their long friendship Viper knew the other man could take him in a fight. Not necessarily because Data was the better fighter, but because his brother was fighting for the only family he had left. It was there in the lines of resolve on his face. He'd beat a motherfucker down and not bat an eyelash for that girl. Viper knew the feeling. "You make her cry, Viper, just one time, I will kill you. Dead. *Very* dead."

"As opposed to being only mostly dead?"

Data gave him an exasperated look before smacking his head. "Fucker."

"I swear I'll protect her. Body and heart, Data. Body and heart."

"You'd better."

Data held out his hand to him and Viper took it. Then Data pulled him in for a quick hug and a slap on the back.

"We good, bro?" Viper asked.

"We're good."

"They're in Las Vegas." Viper pointed to the screen where he'd run a check on credit and debit cards, as well as bank accounts associated with the couple. "Thought they were going to L.A."

"Said that's where they were going. Didn't believe her. She's running. I could hear it in her voice. Always did that when things got hard."

"Well, she didn't run from Mills. They've checked into the Four Seasons. All four of them. At least, four adults with two rooms under his name. Darcy's stepsisters older'n her?"

"Yeah. And I'd tracked them to Vegas. Just hadn't gotten around to finding the hotel."

Viper jerked his head. "Why the hell not? You having second thoughts?"

"No." His answer was instant. Decisive. "I followed the money, so to speak. I didn't want to find them too early because I needed a chance to calm down."

"I take it this is going to be bad."

"The man is a sadistic bastard. Don't know about abuse to his own daughters, but he's definitely into some shady shit." He clasped his hands behind his neck, scrubbing the back of his head several times before continuing. "Darcy's eighteen. His daughters are nineteen. Twins. They've been with Mills since their mother's death when they were sixteen." Viper got a chill down his spine. "There have been regular infusions of cash for him since his wife passed. About once a quarter or so. Large infusions. The last one coming right after Darcy ran off. From a bank in L.A."

"No one's that fucking stupid," Viper denied instantly.

"Donna is. At least, she probably didn't consider I'd look into anything. She was telling me the truth because I could always tell when she was lying."

"Spell this out for me, Data. Because I'm not sure I believe what I'm hearing. It sounds like a bit farfetched."

"I'm still looking. But I've tracked the money from that bank in L.A. to a long-time, if not prominent, U.S. Representative. One of those who holds on to his seat by the skin of his teeth every year and only because higher-ups in the party buy the election for him so they have someone in their pocket to control however they need to."

"Don't say it, Data…"

"I think he's selling his daughters as prostitutes."

"Didn't I just tell you *not* to fuckin' say it?" He sighed, scrubbing a hand over his face. This was fucking bullshit they didn't need. "What do we do now? We can't leave them there."

"I'll give the information to Cain. I'm still trying to confirm my suspicions, and that's going to be hard to do. Fortunately, I have an ace in the hole who's ever better than I am."

"Better than you? Did that hurt to admit?"

Data shot him an annoyed look. "The fuck you talkin' about? Of *course* it hurt!"

They both laughed.

* * *

Darcy wandered outside the compound. Snow crunched under her feet, and the crisp December air cleared her head. What was she doing here? She wanted to get to know her father, but she wasn't nearly as brave as she'd led him to believe. The thought of facing her mother and that son of a bitch she'd married, looking them in the eye, and laying out what that bastard had done to her was daunting. Not so much because she was afraid of either of them -- her father had a scary side to him she didn't ever want to cross -- but because it was highly humiliating and utterly disgusting. Who wanted to relive something like that? Unfortunately, she had nowhere else to go. And she still felt like she owed it to Data to deliver as promised. If he got her parents here, she'd do what she had to do. She'd stand up and be a daughter he was proud of.

Which lead to her other issue. When had her loyalties swung so firmly in Data's corner? Not that she'd ever side herself with her mother, but why him? She didn't know him. The second the question popped into her head, she knew the answer and was ashamed for even asking the question of herself. Data had come after her. Maybe not himself, but he'd sent the most qualified people for the job even though he'd wanted to go himself. Then he'd looked out for her with Viper. And her mother.

Viper.

Why couldn't she stop thinking about him? She had a father to get to know. A club who had essentially taken her in as one of their own. There was so much she needed to do. So many people she needed to learn about. Why was she consumed with a man who would only break her heart?

"Darcy."

Oh, God. She couldn't face him right now.

"Not ready to talk to you yet," she said. "Got stuff to do." She wasn't going to turn around and look at him. Instead, she leaned her forearms against the railing of the fence lining the driveway. One booted foot rested on the bottom rung.

"I'm sorry," he said bluntly. "Not gonna try to gloss it over. I acted like an ass."

She shrugged. "No worries. Consider it history."

"Look at me."

"I told you I'm busy. Can you not accept that and move on?"

"No."

"Why the fuck not? Seemed like you had plenty of company earlier. Go find someone who wants you around, 'cause that ain't me."

"Then why'd you notice I was with another woman?"

Bastard.

When she didn't answer, he placed a hand on her shoulder. Darcy flinched, but didn't pull away. She wasn't giving him that kind of power. If she did, he'd just try to take more. "We're going to talk, and you're going to give me a chance to earn your trust."

With a little huff, she turned to face him and then wished she hadn't. The man just had to be insufferably gorgeous in an unconventional, bad-boy kind of way. He was everything she needed to stay away from, but everything that attracted her. It wasn't the bad-boy thing either. He was strong, protective, and deadly. The exact kind of man who could protect her from people like Rayburn and her mother. Unfortunately, he wasn't the man to do it. At least, not without breaking her heart in the process.

"Look. You said you're sorry. I accepted. What the fuck more do you want from me?"

He stepped close to her, his hands resting on her hips. With little more effort than he'd use lifting a child, he picked her up and sat her on the fence. "I want a chance to start over."

"Start what over?" She was beginning to panic a little. Not because she was afraid of him in the physical sense. She knew she was safe with him. He was the one to drag her ass out of the woods and back to civilization. Back to a place where she was beginning to realize she could sleep soundly and not fear waking up with some sleaze bag standing over her...

"Us, Darcy. Start us over."

"There is no 'us,' Viper. You're the man my daddy warned me about. Literally." She tried to sound flippant, but he slid between her spread thighs, his arms going around her to hold her to him, so that anything she said came out breathless.

"No," he admitted. "There's no us *now*. But there will be."

She shivered. Not from the cold. God, he smelled good! Crisp winter air with evergreen and pine and just... hot, sexy *man*. Was there really any way for her to resist him? What woman could?

"I'm not one of your biker groupies. What do you call them?"

"Patch chasers?" He grinned at her. A slow, sexy grin. "No. You're not. No one gets you but me, Darcy. I'm makin' you my woman. You're mine to protect and keep."

"I see." She didn't, but it didn't really matter. "Tell you what. I think we've both got an itch to scratch. Let's get this over with. After we've fucked, we'll see where we stand."

He actually growled at her, his grip on her tightening until they were mashed together almost seamlessly. "You think you'll fuck me then leave me?"

She shrugged. "Maybe. I may not like sex with you. You're quite a bit older than me. We probably aren't compatible sexually anyway."

Viper urged her even closer to him, until he was pressed firmly between her legs. With his big palm, he urged her to rock against him, putting friction on her clit in just the way she needed. An instantaneous surge of pleasure exploded through her. Not enough to make her climax, but just enough to make her wet in a rush of heat. Darcy couldn't contain her gasp.

"Not compatible? Oh, I think not, Lil' Bit. I think you'll enjoy my brand of sex very much."

"What about Data? You know he's pissed at you." Darcy tried to keep her composure, tried not to let him see how he was affecting her, but knew it was a hopeless battle. This was an experienced man. One who knew exactly what he was doing to a woman. Currently, he was engaging her in a battle she had no hope of winning. One of pleasure. Sex. Sin.

"Data and I have worked things out." He flashed her that fucking cocky-ass grin of his that melted her panties. "He pulled a gun on me. Actually held it to my fuckin' forehead."

"Yet here you are?"

"Some things are just worth the risk."

When his lips met hers in the cold breeze, Darcy felt anything but chilled. His body enveloped hers, his arms trapping her though she didn't fight. Couldn't fight. She kissed him back with everything inside her, all the passion she had. Regardless of knowing he'd never be faithful to her, she couldn't deny she wanted this. Wanted Viper. In her bed. In her body. She just had to keep him out of her heart.

Her fingers found the leather of his jacket. His colors. God, her life had gone so sideways it wasn't even funny. She was actually in the middle of a motorcycle club. Was the daughter of a respected member. She had no idea what a real family felt like, but she'd definitely been welcomed here like she never had with her mother or any of her stepfathers. These men circled the wagons around the people they cared about and, for some reason, they'd included her in that group.

Finally, she just shut down. Let him take her over. She kissed him back, slipped her tongue inside his mouth to take his taste inside her. She inhaled, that warm, masculine scent enveloping her. Hard muscles beneath his jacket bunched against her fingers. Needy growls sang to her. She was surrounded by Viper, by his masculinity. His power. It was a defining moment in her life because she realized that, in no uncertain terms, a part of her would always belong to Viper.

* * *

Getting back to his room was a whirlwind. He took her in the back because the kids were in the great room, but Viper longed to make a public statement for his brothers with her. Let them know what was going on so they'd be aware she was his. Instead, he took the back stairs two at a time with Darcy in his arms. She wasn't passive either. Where before she'd curled her little fingers in his colors, now she twined them in the hair at his neck. Her lips trailed kisses up and down his face until she finally settled at his pulse point and just sucked, leaving her mark on him. Viper wanted to howl in satisfaction.

Once inside his bedroom, he kicked the door shut and set Darcy on her feet long enough to whip her sweater off her luscious body. Wild red hair cascaded over her pale body like a cloak. He pulled off his colors to drape carefully over the back of a chair, but whipped his T-shirt off in one smooth motion and dropped it on the floor. She had barely gotten her jeans unbuttoned and halfway down her thighs when Viper pulled her back to him, lifting her into his arms once again to take her to bed.

Lying there on his big bed, all that red hair spread out around her, she looked like some pale goddess offered up to him. There was a dazed expression on her face, like she wasn't exactly sure how she'd gotten there, but she licked her lips, eyeing him hungrily, letting Viper know she was exactly where she wanted to be.

"Once we do this, Darcy, there's no takin' it back. I'm not gonna to have you only to lose you."

She cocked her head. "Are you always so chatty during sex? Because, I gotta tell you, I'd like a little more action on your part."

Viper bared his teeth at her, everything primal in him rising to her bait. "You want action? Finish stripping. You're not nearly naked enough." She complied while he did the same. Though he regretted not doing it himself, Viper wasn't certain he could have done it without simply ripping her underwear from her little body. It didn't help to have her do it for him. That little thatch of red curls glistening with her arousal didn't help his control. It taunted him to taste. To plunge into her and leave his seed to mix with her own juices.

He must have growled or something because she whimpered, her hands balling into fists at her side.

Those clear, blue eyes widened in alarm, but she didn't try to move away from him. Instead she reached for him, her hand landing on his abs when he planted a knee on the bed and lowered himself over her.

Viper's larger body pressed her into the mattress as he settled himself between her legs. One luscious breast called to him with its rosy peak, and Viper didn't even try to resist. His lips closed over her nipple and Darcy gave a sharp cry, arching into him. Her body was so small, so lithe he groaned with every movement of her skin beneath him. And the little hellion squirmed as she tightened her grip on him. Her legs circled his body and she dug her heels into him, pulling herself against him. Rubbing her pussy over his belly to get friction to heir clit.

"Witch," he hissed around a nipple before moving to the other one to give a hard suck. "Needy little thing."

Sweat dotted her skin, making her move against him with ease. The contrast between his hair-roughened and her silky-smooth flesh was erotic. Viper skimmed his fingers down her side to her hip, where he dug in and attempted to hold her still.

He had to get her under control if he was going to get himself there because never in his life had he experienced such a demanding female. Not in an overly aggressive way either. She didn't tell him what to do or even try to take what she wanted. She was just genuinely out of control, needing something only he could give her. She writhed beneath him, whimpering with every contact of her clit on his belly. He'd wanted to take his time, to introduce her to sex with him carefully. But what had started with a mad dash from the driveway to his bedroom hadn't slowed down at all.

"Hold still," he snapped. In response, she pulled him up to her for a kiss, sliding her tongue against his in a sensual glide. She moaned into his mouth as if he were a delicious treat she couldn't get enough of. "Fuck." He gave up.

Reaching for the dresser beside the bed, he opened the drawer and snagged a condom. He barely managed to roll it over his aching cock before she was reaching for him, guiding him to her wet little cunt.

"Viper," she breathed. She looked up at him, her blue eyes bright with lust and need. She looked so innocent but acted like a wanton. Viper was caught between the desire to give her what she wanted and the need to know how much she could take.

"How many lovers have you had?" The question came out harsher than he intended, but he was on the verge of losing himself in her quivering body and a primal need to punish any man who'd touched her before him.

"I -- one," she said, confusion tempering some of her lust.

"Fuck," he swore again. Sweat broke out over his body as he shook his head to clear it. She'd maneuvered his cock to her entrance where the head had just pressed against her. He was inches away from heaven but was terrified of hurting her.

"What? So I'm not a virgin. Big deal!" She blushed from her cheeks to the roots of her lovely hair, to her breasts, her skin hot with either anger or embarrassment, Viper didn't know which.

"Stop squirming!" He put every ounce of command into his words, needing her to stop wiggling before he came without even entering her.

"Let me up!"

"Woman, stop it!"

"You stop it!" she screamed at him, tears brimming where before there had been only a dazed gleam.

Viper took a calming breath, not moving off her in any way. His cock ached like a motherfucker, but he didn't enter her either.

"I need to know how much you can take, Lil' Bit," he managed to get out. "I don't want to hurt you. One lover, while much preferred to fifty, might not be enough for you to take me."

She lifted her chin but settled beneath him. "We had a lot of sex, big guy. I've only had one lover, but I'm far from inexperienced."

The second the words he needed to hear left her lips, Viper slid into her as far as he could go. She gasped, her lovely eyes widening, but there was no pain on her face. She was tight. *Too* tight. But she didn't seem to be in any discomfort.

That settled, Viper moved inside her. Slow, steady strokes at first. Then faster. Deeper. Darcy met him thrust for thrust, raising her hips to meet him, digging her heels into his ass to urge him to move faster.

It wasn't long before Viper panted as he pummeled into Darcy, the feel of her gripping sheath threatening to unman him.

"Fucking hot little piece," he growled. "Trying to take my cum before I'm ready?" She whimpered, her nails scoring his back like little spurs. "That's it, Lil' Bit. Tell me what you want."

"Fuck me," she whispered. "Oh, God, fuck me hard, Viper!"

"You need to come? You want to milk me dry?"

"Yes! Oh, God!" Her words were punctuated by the slapping of skin on skin as Viper fucked her.

He crushed her to him, needing to get closer. No matter how tightly he held her, no matter how much of her skin touched his, it wasn't enough. Would never be enough. Viper had known she would be an addiction for him, but never thought it would be this all-consuming. His need of her was something he knew in his soul would never be quenched. He would always be Darcy's as long as he lived. No other woman would do for him, and he didn't even want to try.

Her cries grew louder, her nails digging deeper into his skin, the bite of pain an erotic stimulus. "Do it, Lil' Bit," he whispered to her, the devil in her ear. "Give me your cum. Do it! Do it!"

She did. She gave a shrill scream, and her limbs tightened around him nearly as much as her cunt gripped his cock. Her contractions rocked him, threatened to steal his control. He'd intended to let her have her orgasm, and then slow down a little and take her the way she deserved, but the second her pussy gripped his cock in a stranglehold as she came on him, Viper knew it was over.

He held out until the last spasm released her, and then Viper shouted his own orgasm. His cock throbbed inside her in hard, aching pulses as he emptied himself into the condom. Both of them were breathing hard, sweat now cooling their heated skin. Both were clinging to each other. Viper nuzzled her neck, kissing and licking her pulse, praising her body for the pleasure it had given him.

Neither said a word, simply lay there with Viper still buried inside her. She didn't try to push him off her; rather, she still clung to him. It gratified Viper to know she didn't want him to leave her. He knew she'd soon be uncomfortable though.

Carefully, he withdrew and pulled off the condom. She whimpered against him, her limbs loosening from around him, reluctantly slow. Viper knotted the condom and tossed it into the wastebasket beside the bed. He pulled her with him to one side while he fought to get the covers turned down. When he finally managed it, he got them both between the sheets and pulled Darcy snug against him. Her fingers curled into his shoulder, still clinging sweetly to him, but she didn't say a word.

"You OK?" he finally asked. If he'd hurt her…

"I'm wonderful," she sighed. "I've never… Viper, that was so wonderful."

Viper wanted to pound his chest and howl to the ceiling. "Good." So much for the suave, experienced older guy he was. He had no words for her. Not now when he was so raw with the pleasure he'd experienced with her. Instead of speaking more, he kissed her forehead and held her close.

After a while she asked in a drowsy voice, "Will you be here when I wake up?"

"I will, Lil' Bit. I'll be right here with you."

He wasn't certain if she heard him answer because her breathing was even and deep. Fast asleep in his arms.

Where she belonged.

Chapter Six

Darcy woke, screaming as an incredible orgasm seized her body. She was naked on her back, her legs spread with Viper's dark head buried between them. He growled and snarled, slurping loudly as she continued to come helplessly.

"Viper!" Her hand flew to his head where she'd intended to push him away. Instead she found her fingers curling in his hair, holding him to her as she ground herself on his mouth.

"Jesus, you taste good," he snarled. "Never get enough of this." When she shuddered, whimpering before she could stop herself, he flashed her a decidedly wicked grin. "Come for me, Lil' Bit. I want to hear you scream again."

She did. Long. Loud.

Darcy took a much-needed gulp of air, finally pushing Viper away and closing her legs slightly, whimpering, "No more. Give me a second."

He crawled up her body, forcing her knees open before blanketing her with his bigger frame. When he kissed her, she tasted herself on his lips. His tongue. She clung to him, her nails digging into his back as she held him to her. He was an incredible lover, way beyond her experience. This was more than mere lust. It was raw. Primitive.

Unable to contain the sensations building inside her, Darcy surrendered to Viper. He was the one in control. Anything he wanted, she would give him willingly. It never occurred to her she should resist him, that the very earth-shattering pleasure she craved from him was a direct result of his vast experience where she had relatively little. Before Viper, sex had been pleasant. Fun. This was an all-consuming burn she had no hope of containing.

Somehow, Viper had put on a condom. She knew not because she saw him, but because she felt the barrier between them when he slid inside her. One arm was securely around her while he rested most of his weight on the other one until he was firmly seated inside her. Then he wrapped the other arm around her and found her lips with his once more.

There were no other words between them, only the steady, erotic slide of their bodies speaking for them. Darcy knew this was a moment that would change her forever. She had no idea if she actually loved Viper. She didn't think so. Not yet. But she knew she'd forever crave his touch. No other man would ever be able to satisfy her in bed.

The breath left her lungs in little staccato gasps in time to his jarring thrusts into her body. Whimpers escaped, and she didn't even try to hold them back. He seemed to purr deep in his chest, his satisfaction with her radiating out from the inside as she felt those little growls through him where she was mashed so wonderfully against him.

The moonlight filtered gently through the curtains so his eyes glimmered down at her when he raised his head. There was definite lust shining there, but also a possessiveness that took her breath away. She swallowed as he continued to move inside her with slow but powerful strokes. The rhythm of his body was as mesmerizing as the carnal look in his eyes.

"You're mine, Darcy," he whispered. "You know you are." All she could do was stare at him, wide-eyed, much like a kitten might look at a hawk bearing down on it. "You'll stay here with me. You'll let me protect you. You'll confront your mother and stepfather only when I tell you to. When you do, you will look to me for strength when you need it." When all she did was stare up at him, he stopped moving, making her tilt her hips for more. He stayed her with his big hand griping her ass. "Want an answer, Lil' Bit." When she only nodded he rolled them slightly so he could deliver a stinging swat to her butt cheek. "A verbal answer."

"Yes," she managed to squeak. "I… yes."

"Yes what?"

The sensations were so much her mind was muddled. "What was the question?"

He grinned at her, caressing the little smack he'd given her ass. "Just say you're mine and I'll let it go. For now."

"I'm yours, Viper." Her voice was a breathy sigh as she arched her back so her nipples once again rubbed along his hair-roughened chest. "Just…"

"What, Lil' Bit? Just what?"

"Don't break my heart." She made the little demand in almost a whisper. She was giving entirely too much away but couldn't seem to help it. She wanted Viper. Wanted to belong to him. And him to her. But how did she communicate that without sounding clingy? He probably had women like this all the time. She, with her one lover, was a rank novice.

Instead of answering her, he started moving again, this time rolling them over so that he surged up inside her while she lay on top of him. His bent knees placed his feet solidly on the mattress and he used the leverage to power inside of her with seemingly little effort. She cried out weakly as an orgasm washed over her. Viper's big arms circled her body, holding her to him tightly as he pumped into her again and again.

Finally, he let out a long, strangled groan, his cock throbbing inside her as he emptied himself. A small part of her regretted it hadn't been inside her pussy instead of the condom, but that was just crazy. She was caught up in the moment. Yet, both times they'd had sex, it had been Viper who had remembered to protect them both. What did that say about her?

With one last squeeze, Viper rolled them back over, slipping out of her as he did. He kissed her temple, her forehead, her eyelids before settling on her lips for several long moments. Then he removed the condom and disposed of it in the wastebasket beside the bed before pulling her into his arms once again.

"Nearly time for me to go. You sleep as long as you need to. When you're rested, come to the common room. There's always somethin' to eat."

"Where are you going?" Darcy bit her lip as soon as she'd asked the question. It wasn't her business, and they both knew it. Instead of scowling at her, he gave her a cocky little grin before answering.

"Have to meet with the rest of the club. See if they found anything new on your folks."

"Did you find them?"

"Oh, yeah. We're resourceful like that."

She wanted to ask where they were, but decided it didn't matter. They were there. She was here. As she preferred it.

"Look, Lil' Bit. I'll keep you in the loop as much as I can. They're currently in Vegas, and we think your mother and stepfather are selling your stepsisters as prostitutes."

Darcy gasped. She'd always been so caught up in her own problems she hadn't even thought about whether or not the older girls were going through their own problems. "I never even considered that. Oh, God!"

"Does it surprise you?" He looked at her carefully, waiting her answer.

Darcy took her time, really thinking about her time with the other girls. "I wasn't around them much. We lived in the same house, but I mostly kept myself barricaded in my room so I didn't have to deal with anyone." She shrugged helplessly. "No? I guess it doesn't really surprise me, but I never paid any attention to them. They're older than me, but not by much. A year. Maybe two. This is awful! How could I not have seen it?"

"Because you were trying to look out for yourself? Let it go, baby. This isn't your fault and I refuse to let you feel like it is." He kissed her gently. "I'll keep you informed. If I have to leave to help retrieve them, you'll stay here with your dad. He'll look out for you when I can't."

She raised her chin a little. "Do I need looking after? Thought you guys weren't mean to women."

He gave her an impatient look. "We're not. But there are still women here who would love to test you. While I have no doubt you can take care of yourself, I'd feel better if someone specific had your back. Data is the logical choice. Until you learn the rules and the chain of command, you need someone to guide you."

"What rules? What happens if I break one?"

"Are you looking to pick a fight? 'Cause I gotta tell ya, sparring with you makes me hard as a motherfucker. You go against me, I'm gonna be fuckin' you night and day just 'cause of the hard-on it gives me."

Darcy's breath escaped her in a rush. "Oh…" Just that fast, she was turned on beyond belief.

He flashed her a cocky grin, pulling her to him. "Too late."

"Who says I want to fuck you again?"

"No one said you'd be fuckin' me, Lil' Bit." He flipped her over to her stomach as he rolled on another condom. When she automatically went to her knees, Viper shoved her back down, spreading her legs and urging them up so that she lay with her bent knees spread wide and her belly flat on the bed. Viper slid his hands under her knees to pull them even further up until she was completely open to him. His cock found her entrance easily and slid home. He put his mouth right by her ear, whispering wickedly. "But I'll damned sure be fuckin' you."

"Viper," she whimpered, arching her back as best she could to meet his thrusts. He smacked one cheek of her ass.

"Hold still!" When she whimpered again, continuing to move on him, he smacked the other cheek. This time, she cried out but kept arching her back, moving her hips up and down. Riding him shamelessly.

Viper gripped her tiny waist, pulling her so that she was draped over his thighs, her ass slightly in the air, but he took her weight, her legs still spread wide. Once situated the way he wanted, Viper started to fuck Darcy hard, pulling her back onto his cock in vicious yanks. She cried out, her head turned to one side so that her face rested on the mattress. Her arms were bent, her hands curled by her head. Other than the way her face tensed with her cries, her body was completely limp, letting him do as he needed, passive beneath him.

Fuck!

"You're such a little wanton," he growled as he fucked her in ever-increasing intensity. "I think you like it when I spank your ass." To punctuate his statement, he smacked her ass again, the cheek reddening beneath his hand in a satisfactory display. Darcy surprised herself by rewarding him with a gush of moisture, her orgasm hovering just on the edge. "Fuck, woman! Just... *fuck*!"

"Viper," she moaned. "Oh, God! Gonna... gonna come!"

"Do it! Do it, baby! Come all over my cock! Right... fucking... *NOW*!"

She did. Something inside Darcy exploded, her whole being laid bare at Viper's feet. There was no way to hold herself back from him. No way to guard her heart. How could a woman receive such extreme pleasure and be expected to hold herself in check? She knew she certainly couldn't. Whatever he wanted from her body, she'd give it to him because of this one moment. He'd taken her three times. Every single one of them had been a revelation to her. It was more than just sex. To her, it was... *everything*. Viper engaged her entire being when he fucked her. She lost her mind and just let him have whatever he wanted. There hadn't been a second she'd regretted any of it, either. If he left her today, she'd be devastated, but she wouldn't have missed any of this for the entire world.

Viper gritted his teeth, groaning loudly as if he were trying to hold off his own orgasm. The second her cunt ceased contracting around him, he blanketed her body with his and fucked her mercilessly, driving his cock into her with brutal force. Splayed out as she was, Darcy could do nothing but lie there and take the pounding he gave her. And embrace the orgasm washing over her again. Her cries were sharp and sounded as desperate as she felt. The pleasure rushed through her with dizzying force and speed before leaving her completely spent, limp and passive beneath him. When Viper came, it was with a deafening roar to the ceiling. She felt him pulsing inside her, his cum spilling inside the condom, his cock stretching her with each aching throb.

They lay like that for several minutes. His heavy weight pressed her into the mattress. Sweat clung to both of them as a result of their exertions. Viper's breath was heavy in her ear, his beard tickling her shoulder as he kissed and praised her over and over with little nips and licks.

Finally, he groaned and rolled off her, pulling her with him. Again, he curled his arm around her, holding her to him. His big, hair-roughened body was pure magic. He was a big man, all strength and brawn. She felt safe in his arms. Cherished, even. It was a fantasy, she knew, but one she readily embraced.

"What the fuck am I going to do with you, Lil' Bit," he murmured. "You take my breath away."

She had no idea what to say to that. He more than took her breath away. She was already becoming obsessed with him, his loving.

But that was the problem. Lust and love were two different things. If she were going to survive this with her heart intact, she needed to remember that.

Finally, he turned her face to him, kissing her gently. There were so many things that kiss told her, but she was too afraid to read too much into it. For now, she'd take what he gave her and hope it would be enough.

"Rest, baby. I'll be back soon. If you want to go to the common room, I'm sure Suzie would love some help with the decorating. So would the women."

"They're all really nice," she managed. It seemed inane to say, but she was grateful they were treating her well. "Thanks for coming after me. I'd never admit it to my mom, but taking off like I did probably wasn't the smartest thing I've ever done. But I really thought it was necessary. I couldn't stay there another second."

Viper looked at her, seeming to see into her very soul. She wouldn't put it past him and he'd probably succeed, too. She was so raw and stripped bare he probably could see her innermost secrets.

"You gonna tell me what happened?"

"I will. But not until you have them here."

"Why is that important to you? Why not just tell me and let Bones decide what needs to be done? We could save you the unpleasantness of having to face them again."

"That wouldn't be fair. I'll tell you and Data alone before I confront them. But not until you have them and my stepsisters here." She looked away from him, a sudden overwhelming urge to cry blanketing her. "I left them, Viper. I was looking out for myself and didn't even give them the option to go with me. What kind of person does that make me?"

The second she started talking, Viper sat up and pulled her into his arms across his lap. "Look at me, Darcy," he said, that commanding tone back in his voice. "You listen to me and you listen good, baby. *None of this is your fault.* If you'd known, you might have gotten them to go with you, but would they have survived like you did? Five days in the wild? Cold? No fire and little food? Did they even indicate to you they were in trouble? Did they protect you?"

"I guess not, but that's not the point. I should have looked into it more carefully."

"At any time did you think they were in trouble, Darcy? I'm asking you to really think back. When I told you that Rayburn character was selling them into prostitution, you looked as surprised as if I'd slapped you. So, I'm asking you again. Did they give you any indication they were in trouble?"

She tried to pull herself together. Perhaps it was the fact she'd already been stripped bare emotionally. Perhaps she really hadn't seen anything to make her think Rayburn treated his daughters badly. Finally, she just sighed. Defeated. "I honestly don't know. Not that I recall. They were always smiling and laughing, but pretty much kept to themselves. I guess I just didn't look hard enough."

"Or maybe they were embarrassed and didn't want you to look too closely at them," he said softly. "Did you ever think they were just fragile?"

"No. Not like you mean. They were delicate and feminine, but I never looked at them too closely. I was too busy creating havoc for Rayburn and my mother. I hated Rayburn from the second I met him and was right to. He always gave me the creeps. His daughters, however, were just, I don't know. Perfect. Straight A students. Cheerleaders. These beautiful, well-behaved girls everyone envied. They seemed so happy, I never thought it might be an act. Not once. As far as I knew, they were one big happy family."

"Good. Leave it there. After we get the girls, your mother, and their dad here, we'll sort it all out. I can tell you unequivocally, though, you did the right thing. Besides, it all worked out anyway. Data sent us after you. Now, we'll find the rest of them. Your stepsisters will be safe. And we'll deal with the other two."

"Do I want to know?"

"Probably not. And I wouldn't tell you anyway."

"I see." She cleared her throat, trying to shake off the guilt. "Well, I guess I'll just have to make the best of it. If nothing else, I can apologize to Serelda and Winter. Hopefully, they'll understand."

Viper pinched her chin in his thumb and finger, forcing her to look at him. He held her gaze for several seconds, then said, "They will. It will all work out."

Once he left her, Darcy dressed and headed to the common room like he'd told her. Again, she found Stunner sitting in the same chair, same disgruntled look on his face. Glitter was everywhere, clinging to his clothes, beard, and hair, effectively turning him into a life-sized Christmas ornament. Suzie was happily chatting to him while she decorated. Darcy was about to offer to help with other decorations when a young man stomped toward the pair. He wore no identifying patches on his vest other than one that said "Prospect" on the chest.

"You're disrespecting him, Suzie," the guy said. "If another club came in here, Stunner would look like a fool and they'd laugh at all of us for allowing it."

Instantly, Stunner's eyes were on the prospect, his gaze hard and cold.

"I'm just decorating, Pig," Suzie said, her voice not nearly as strong as Darcy had heard her in the past. Clearly, the girl was wary of the prospect. "Stunner didn't say I couldn't."

"You know that fucker never talks! Besides, he lets you do whatever you want. I'm tellin' you, it's time for you to grow the fuck up! Stop actin' like a kid! If you want to stay here, you gotta act your age."

"She's only twelve, Pig." Daniel and Cliff had come up behind the prospect. "She's had it hard. If she wants to be a kid a while longer, no one minds. Especially not Stunner."

"She's a brat! A disgrace to the club!" He turned back to Suzie. "You'll never be any use to anyone here! I don't know why Cain puts up with you! The only thing you'll ever be good at is bein' a whore!"

Stunner stood abruptly, knocking the chair over. He was younger than Data or Viper, but there was a look in his eyes that said he'd seen more than he ever wanted to.

"She's making you look like a fool, Stunner," Pig continued. Darcy winced. She could have told the dumbass he was in over his head, but figured he deserved it for what he'd said to Suzie. Even now, the girl looked beaten down, tears dripping steadily from her lashes as she looked down at the floor. "All that fuckin' glitter. What the fuck, Stunner? You're just sittin' there lettin' her do this to you?"

With no further warning, Stunner launched himself at the prospect, tackling him to the floor. Once he was straddling Pig's supine body with his much bigger one, Stunner proceeded to beat the living fuck out of the man. Blood splattered over the floor with each hit. It happened so fast, Pig didn't have the chance to raise a hand in his defense. Stunner howled to the ceiling in rage before continuing the brutal assault. The veins and tendons stood out starkly, and his eyes were wild, those of an animal on a rampage.

Darcy moved forward, but a woman's hand on her shoulder stopped her. "Don't interfere. The boys will stop it when it's time."

She looked over her shoulder to find a young woman her own age. She was beautiful, but shy. Her long, jet-black hair was straight and hung over one side of her face. When she moved her head slightly to look at the fight -- or, rather, beating -- Darcy noticed a scar beneath the fall of hair that ran over her cheek before disappearing again behind her hair. Darcy could see enough to tell the young woman had tried to cover it with makeup, but it was deep, though completely healed.

"He's going to kill that man," Darcy said.

The woman shrugged. "Isn't as if he doesn't have it coming. Besides, Stunner isn't the first one of us who's wanted to off that bastard."

Darcy looked back at Stunner. There wasn't much left of Pig's face but splintered bone and meat. An older couple who had been introduced to her as Mama and Pops finally pulled Stunner off Pig. Not with muscle, but with gentle hands. No one said anything. Arkham appeared in front of them all, standing over Pig, an unreadable expression on his face.

Stunner was breathing heavily, blood splattered over his clothing, his hands covered with it. He looked at Arkham, the men locking gazes. Arkham sighed, then nodded at Stunner before picking the unconscious prospect up in a fireman's carry and going deeper into the clubhouse. Mama and Pops followed him, but not before Pops hugged little Suzie and ruffled her hair. The girl looked heartbroken.

Stunner met Darcy's gaze, looking back and forth from her to Suzie. He wanted her to stay with the girl. When Darcy nodded, Stunner hurried out of the room.

"Suzie?" Cliff came to her side and laid a hand on her shoulder. "You OK?"

She nodded, not looking at the young man.

"You know Stunner would never hurt you. Right?" Daniel made her look up at him before brushing tears from her face. "He just... well, he doesn't like anyone being mean to you."

She nodded, but said nothing, her gaze returning to the floor.

"Will she be OK?" Darcy had to know. Stunner had beaten a guy senseless right in front of the child.

"She'll be fine," Cliff said. "She's seen worse. At least this time, it wasn't directed at her." He met Darcy's gaze. "That remark about her being a whore? The club we ran from was doing exactly that." He spat on the floor in the direction they'd carted off Pig. "Bastard deserved what he got and more."

Exactly three minutes later, Stunner stomped back to his chair and sat motionless for long moments, his gaze shifting from Suzie to a spot in front of him. He looked to be freshly showered and dressed in clean clothes, his hair still damp, but no longer splattered in blood. Stunner grunted a couple of times, but Suzie didn't move, just stood there with her head down and tears quietly tracking down her lovely face.

Again, Stunner grunted. Louder this time. The man could talk, Darcy had heard him. Apparently, it wasn't the norm.

When Suzie still didn't move, he put one hand on her shoulder and handed her the red glitter with the other, obviously wanting her to continue decorating him. She took the glitter, looking up at him, but didn't do more. Finally, in obvious desperation, Stunner snagged the gold glitter and dumped it over his head, grunting louder.

Finally, finally, the girl gave a faint smile. The longer she looked at the big biker, the wider her grin became until she giggled. The second the sound echoed throughout the room, the entire collective of big, badass bikers seemed to breathe a sigh of relief. Many of them chuckled as they moved about their business again. Stunner tried to look disgruntled, but even he looked relieved. Especially when Suzie dried her eyes, sniffled once, then began to sing Christmas carols softly while continuing her work on his beard with the glitter.

Darcy noticed two things. First, Stunner was completely devoted to Suzie. Not in a romantic or creepy sense -- like Rayburn -- but like a guardian. A protector. God help any boy who decided he wanted to date Suzie. Second, the entire group of men and women in the common room hadn't lifted a finger to help their prospect, but every single one of them without exception were gratified to hear the girl start singing. One of them even turned up the volume of the song she was singing slightly until she matched it. When she was once again singing merrily, every single man on the floor had a wide, affectionate grin on his face. Well, except Stunner. The happier everyone else seemed, the more disgruntled he seemed. Darcy suspected his expression was solely to please Suzie. Like he knew she enjoyed using him as her own personal Christmas ornament only because he was uncomfortable with it and he was determined to keep up his act just to please her.

This club wasn't anything like what she expected. They were a family. A tight family. They looked out for each other and God damn everyone else.

Darcy wanted that for herself.

Chapter Seven

The logistics in going after their targets had proved frustrating for Bones. Viper felt his frustration mounting. It didn't sit well with him to delay in getting an innocent out of danger, but then, his loyalties were divided for the first time in his life. His brothers were just as frustrated, but they didn't have to look their women in the eyes every day and night and tell her they couldn't go after her family yet.

The problem was in the number of MCs in the Vegas area. They didn't want to intrude on another club's territory, but lacked a mediator. Cain had reached out to several, but so far no one was game to have another club on a run inside their territory.

It had been four long days. Not long, but in an operation like this, an eternity. Who knew how long the Mills would be in Vegas? Or how safe those two young women were. Viper, Bohannon, Torpedo, and Cain had had heated debates about what to do. Viper, of course, and Bohannon were all for just riding in and doing what had to be done, but Cain and Torpedo were more level headed, knowing that wouldn't fly. Bones was extremely territorial about its own area. Going into another club's territory without express permission was just not something they were willing to do at this point. None of their own were threatened. Yes, there were innocents involved, but they couldn't save everyone. It was a sore spot with Viper, but he knew Cain was right.

Then came an enemy Bones had established a truce with. Viper didn't know what to think, but anyone who could get them in was welcomed. Depending on what he expected in return, that is.

"You ain't gonna believe this," Arkham said as he gazed out the window. "Do we even have spotters on the grounds anymore? Cause if we do, we got a serious problem."

"Shadow sent a text," Bohannon said, readying a weapon and tossing another one to Cain. "Not sure what happened to the others, but we'll be finding out." He glanced up at Cain, his expression hard as granite. "That fucker has balls the size of Texas, I'll give him that."

"We sure it's him?"

"Unless you know of someone else who'd ride into this country in a white stretch Rolls Royce limousine, yeah."

Cain shook his head and gave an exasperated sigh. "Fucker." He raised his voice. "Sword, might want to get your woman out of the common area. Her daddy's paying a visit."

El Diablo was somewhat of an enigma. He'd been a top enforcer of sorts in the upper echelon of organized crime over the world. During the beginning of his career, he'd met Magenta's mother and begun an affair with her during which Magenta was conceived. They'd reached an uneasy truce when they'd last encountered El Diablo. So why was the fucker here now?

A few seconds later, the elegant limousine Bohannon referred to pulled up nearly to the front door. Right behind it were two large food trucks emblazoned with "Machiallo's Cuisine" on the side in big red letters. After that, several bikes followed, parking so that they flanked both the truck and the limousine. Every biker wore his colors proudly. Which meant they were here on business representing their club. El Diablo was impeccably dressed, as always, in a dark, charcoal-colored suit with a bright green tie. Fucker even had a little gem-encrusted Santa as a lapel pin.

"Greetings, Bones!" His boisterous welcome was out of place given he had just waltzed into another club's home turf. "I bring Christmas cheer to my daughter and her family!"

Cain, Torpedo, Bohannon, and Viper stepped outside onto the porch. Sword stayed inside with Magenta, his ol' lady. Unfortunately, Magenta was also El Diablo's daughter. The man had been looking for ways to get Bones to accept him into their fold even though he'd taken over his own club, Black Reign, out of Florida.

"What do you want, El Diablo?" Cain opted for the straightforward approach. Viper had learned from their previous encounters directness usually worked best with the other man. Though El Diablo had lived in Great Britain for a time, he hadn't adopted the English trait of circling around the problem to find the path of least resistance, or the most diplomatic path. Though he was always unfailingly polite -- until he wasn't -- he appreciated bluntness. Viper thought it was one of the things he found fascinating about Bones. They never bowed to him, no matter they knew the power he wielded.

"Only to give my daughter and her newly found family a Merry Christmas."

"Not Christmas yet," Bohannon said, stepping in front of Cain to better protect him if things went sideways.

"Of course not," El Diablo said, chuckling. "I know all of you likely have your Christmas all planned out. I simply wanted to give something to everyone, and this was the best thing I knew to do." He waved at the catering trucks, a large, friendly smile on his face.

More of Bones' members filed out, curious now they were pretty sure there wasn't going to be a fight.

"What's 'Machiallo's?' Ain't from Somerset." One of the prospects, Kickstand, ventured closer to the Black Reign group, eyeing the offering with open interest.

"Machiallo's is owned by me. I employ only the finest chefs, who prepare only the finest foods." El Diablo lifted his chin and puffed out his chest proudly. "I have brought you a feast fit for a king."

"Guess you don't half do nothin,' do ya?" Sword leaned against the doorframe, blocking Magenta from leaving the clubhouse. She pushed past him anyway. He growled at her, but Viper noted he didn't stop her. Not something he'd be able to manage himself in Sword's position.

"If something isn't worth doing right, it's not worth doing. My daughter is certainly worth every penny spent."

"El Diablo," Magenta said, stepping forward a little. "I think what the boys are dancing around is, while we appreciate the gift," she looked up nervously at Sword. The large man smiled at her, nodding his approval as his hand reached to run the length of her long, blonde hair down her back to settle possessively on her hip. "We'd like to know what you expect in return."

El Diablo actually looked taken aback. "Nothing, my dear. This is a gift. No strings attached. I merely want to wish you all a Merry Christmas. Is that so hard to accept?" He looked both amused and humble, neither of which seemed to fit the man himself. With his dark good looks and charming, charismatic personality, he normally looked anything but humble.

"Uh huh." Cain didn't looked convinced, but he stepped off the wide porch to greet El Diablo properly. Bohannon shadowed him closely, his eyes on the men around them.

Cain reached out a hand in greeting, which El Diablo took with a delighted chuckle. "Merry Christmas, brother. May our two clubs co-exist in harmony in the coming year."

"Merry Christmas to you, too. But you have to know I got no intention of giving you permission to open up drug traffic through Somerset. It's been difficult to wean the area off the flow of drugs coming from the south, but I believe the results are worth it."

"You still have problems, Cain. People are still getting their drugs."

"I'm aware of that. So are the dealers. But they're having to work harder for it. My hope is, most of them will follow their supply."

"Isn't that a little like robbing Peter to pay Paul? Just shuffle the problem somewhere else?"

"Absolutely." Cain didn't bother denying it. "But then it becomes someone else's problem, and my territory is clean."

El Diablo laughed, clapping Cain on the back like they were old friends. "I knew there was a reason I liked you. Come. Invite us in. We eat, then I bring some business for you." When Cain opened his mouth to deliver what Viper was sure was a scathing reply, El Diablo raised his hands. "Nothing to do with drugs. In fact, nothing to do with Black Reign at all. But I might be able to help you with a problem." He grinned wide. "As my Christmas gift to you."

Everything in Viper stilled. He wanted to press the other man, but El Diablo had already started directing the caterers. Viper looked to Cain, who had gone stony-faced. Viper looked at the other officers in Bones, and could see none of them liked the situation. Normally, Cain would have told El Diablo to fuck off and take the food with him, but they all wanted to hear what he had to say. In their own clubhouse, they felt better about the situation, like they could better control things if they went sideways.

Cain nodded to Arkham, who took Deadeye and Goose. The three of them disappeared into the interior of the clubhouse. Viper knew they'd post up where they had a good view of the area and could keep a target on El Diablo and the men he'd brought with him. The man Viper was most looking for was Rycks. The man seemed to be El Diablo's personal guard but he was nowhere to be seen. Which meant he was around somewhere doing the same thing Arkham was doing to the other members of Black Reign.

Watch your six, Viper sent to Arkham and the others in a group text, knowing the man would be in constant communication with Cain that way as well as with the bugs they had planted all over the common room for just such an occasion. *Rycks is missing. He's never been far from El Diablo when we encountered them before.*

10-4, Arkham texted back.

The man had definitely brought a feast. Apparently, Black Reign had nothing on the Whos of Whoville when it came to a Christmas feast. There was turkey, ham, and pork loin, all fixed various ways. The pork loin with some kind of sweet, spice accent with sweet potatoes. The turkey, of course, came stuffed and was so tender it nearly fell apart when touched to carve it. The ham was a country ham, salty and cooked to perfection. There were dishes Viper had no clue what they were, but also some seasonal favorites like corn pudding and a sweet potato pie that would make Patti LaBelle weep. El Diablo had also brought so many different kinds of bread they'd be bloated for a month. Not only were there crescent and split-top rolls, but there was spoon bread, corn bread, sourdough bread, and a couple different sweet breads that went well with dessert. Which was a meal in itself.

The feast went on, literally, for three hours. The men from Bones, while protective of the women and children, relaxed and mingled with their counterparts from Black Reign. Cain and El Diablo talked openly both about business and life in general. All in all, it was relaxing, even with the specter that was El Diablo hovering over them all.

The children had their own table. Surprisingly, Black Reign had brought their women and children as well. The adults mingled at the huge, long table in the common room used for when the club entertained, which was often. The children chatted happily along, eating their fill then adjourning to the activity room to play video games. The whole thing was nearly surreal, like they were just one big happy family enjoying the holidays.

The only adult who didn't sit with the adults was Stunner. The huge young man was right there at Suzie's side, ever the protective beast who never left his master. At least, that was how Viper thought of it. Because, really, the girl said hop and the man jumped, not even asking how high. He couldn't discourage the big guy because, since he'd taken up guard duty, little Suzie had really come out of her shell. She still had nightmares, from what Angel told them all, but

Stunner was always the one at her side to soothe her. He'd taken to sleeping outside her door so much that they'd gotten him a room right across the hall from Suzie. Both left their doors open, and Stunner was sensitive to her every whimper or cry. The two seemed almost symbiotic. Right now, he sat at the table, eating as hard as he ever did, with red, green, and gold glitter all in his face and beard. Suzie had introduced him as her "very best friend in the whole wide world."

Arkham had been in constant, steady contact with the officers. Their earpieces proved invaluable during moments like these. As a result, they were able to seem relaxed when they were all on high alert, just waiting for the word from Arkham or the silent sentinels keeping watch over them.

"Still an all clear," Arkham said softly for them all. "Rycks is holed up with a couple of his men outside the compound keeping watch, but they don't look to be doing more than that. Want me to invite them inside?"

Viper looked at Cain, who looked for all the world as if he were engrossed in whatever El Diablo was saying. And he could likely repeat every single word the man was saying. Viper knew he was also formulating a reply for Arkham.

Cain took a pull from his beer, never taking his eyes off El Diablo. "Tell me something,"

"Anything," the man said, his familiar menacing drawl firmly in place. On anyone else it would have sounded like a veiled threat. This was simply the way El Diablo sounded.

"Why do you have your best men watching us instead of joining the party?"

El Diablo didn't miss a beat, but simply smiled and chuckled. "You don't miss much, do you?"

"It's how I keep us all safe," Cain answered, saying nothing more but instead waiting for El Diablo to answer. The table had gone quiet as if everyone had just been waiting for Cain to call the other man out. Black Reign men tensed, but didn't make any aggressive moves. Bones did the same.

"Just so." El Diablo put his hands flat on the table. "Rycks, bring everyone inside. Warm yourself and fill your bellies."

"They're on the move," Arkham confirmed. "Leaving their weapons in their vehicles and moving on foot. ETA ten minutes."

"Are we going to get to the real reason for your visit?" Viper was glad Cain took this break in the celebration to acknowledge the pink elephant in the room. The sooner they got this over with, the better he'd feel.

"It has come to my attention you're looking for a certain couple in Las Vegas."

Viper went tense, on the alert. Data too. The man would take it personally that anyone had been able to follow his trail on the net.

Cain wiped his mouth, taking his time in answering. "We are." He nodded toward Darcy. "The couple is her mother and stepfather. Two young women with them are her stepsisters. Do you have information about any of them?"

El Diablo nodded, his mien turning serious. "I do." He looked at Darcy with something like genuine pity in his expression. "I'm sure I don't need to inform you that the couple are not the most... wholesome of people."

Darcy ducked her head. Viper could feel her slight body trembling where his thigh was pressed firmly against hers. "No, sir," she said softly. She looked up then. Viper wanted to warn her to keep silent, but she had every right to ask her own questions. This wasn't a formal meeting of clubs. This was a holiday gathering among friends. At least, that was the impression El Diablo wanted to present. "Do you know if Serelda and Winter are OK?"

"They are safe at the moment. Mills and his wife left them in the company of an associate of mine. The man has promised to keep them safe until I give him further instructions."

"Is this the reason you came here?" Magenta's angry outburst brought all attention to her. "To threaten to hurt those young women if Cain doesn't give you whatever it is you want?"

A wince of pain actually crossed El Diablo's face before he answered his daughter. "Of course not, sweetheart. I sincerely came here to offer the information I had. No strings attached." He sighed. "That's not entirely true. I'd hoped to use it as a gesture of good will toward you. I want nothing more than to be part of your life." He put down his napkin and took a deep breath. "Whether or not you agree to open a dialogue with me, Magenta, I'm offering the girls to Bones on the condition they be given the choice of what to do once they've gotten back on their feet. My contact says they are in relatively good health, but their trust is in tatters. If Bones doesn't want the responsibility, Black Reign will assume care of the pair."

Magenta opened her mouth but El Diablo cut her off. "And by care I mean just that. They will be protected from anyone and everyone. No one will prey on them ever again." He clapped his hands together as if closing a deal. "So, if little Darcy there wants her sisters with her, she has them. The mother and father…" He trailed off. "I'm giving you the privilege of giving them what they so obviously deserve. If you don't feel you can carry out the justice needed, I'll happily take them with me. No fuss. No muss. No strings. And nothing leading back to Bones at all."

Cain was silent for long, long moments. The tension stretched out so strong Viper thought he could cut it with a knife. "You'd do this out of the goodness of your heart? Pardon me if I seem skeptical, but generosity doesn't seem to be in your character. Not like this."

El Diablo didn't smile. He looked like the legend they'd found a few months ago in Florida. "You're right. I'm not an overly generous person. Especially with business. I give you the choice of taking them or not because your man, Viper, is with Donna's daughter. I suspect the woman's husband abused her in some way, though I didn't press to find out as the young woman is not my responsibility. Winter and Serelda, however, I will be responsible in getting justice for. Assuming there is anything left after Darcy has her justice."

"You mean kill them," Darcy said, her voice a thread of sound. "Don't you?"

"I'm afraid so, my dear. At least that would seem the sentence for Rayburn. As to your mother, I'd have to know her involvement before I took action. At the very least, she went along with whatever Rayburn had planned for you and his own daughters. Which, really, is enough for me not to lose sleep over disposing of her."

Darcy looked at Viper, going to him for guidance, complete trust in her eyes. "What do you think?"

Viper wanted to howl with the rightness of it. "It will be much easier on you to let El Diablo and his men deal with this."

She looked at the other man. "Would I have to tell you what happened to me?"

El Diablo shook his head. "We have enough on Rayburn we wouldn't need anything else. I'm sure we can get enough from the two young women to determine the severity of Donna's punishment."

Darcy sighed before looking at Viper. Her chin was up, that stubborn look she got that shot his cock hard as granite on her lovely face. "No. I need to confront them both, too. If Winter and Serelda have to, then I can do it as well. For my own peace of mind. I'm not naive enough to think you or Bones will just turn them over to the authorities, so I'm torn between Bones being responsible for whatever happens to them and just letting someone else take them out and bury them." She looked to Cain. "This seems to me like a club matter. I'll defer to you and Bones in this."

Nothing in his life could possibly have made Viper prouder in that moment. His woman had fully accepted his world. More, she accepted her place in it.

Cain looked just as proud of her as Viper did. He raised his head in acknowledgement, looking at his ol' lady, Angel. He pulled Angel's hand to his mouth and kissed the backs of her knuckles. "We'll accept responsibility for all four of them," Cain said without hesitation. "Name your terms."

"There are none. I would hope my daughter would consider opening a place in her life for me, but it's by no means a requirement. As to Bones and Black Reign, I believe we could benefit each other, but again, it's not necessary. Only a humble request."

"You should know, though we do occasionally accept contraband traffic in our area, there are certain things we don't touch. Just as I'm trying to shut down the drug trafficking through Somerset, human trafficking is on the blacklist as well."

"We could discuss any future endeavors thoroughly. I only wish for you to keep us in mind. Should the time ever come when we ask for assistance, I'd hope we could count on Bones to give it serious consideration."

Cain stood, sticking out his hand. "That I can promise you. I don't consider Black Reign allies, but I will no longer consider you an enemy."

"Truce then," El Diablo said as he stood and grasped Cain's hand in a firm handshake.

"Truce."

"Well, then. Our business is concluded. I have presents for the little ones. And for my daughter."

Viper had no idea what those presents were because he snagged Darcy's hand, leading her out of the common room as he made some lame excuses. He needed her. Desperately.

As it turned out, she needed him too.

Chapter Eight

Two days later, El Diablo made another appearance. This time, he had Rayburn and Donna Mills and their two daughters in tow. The two girls looked terrified beyond belief, but the man escorting them was gentle with them. He didn't do more than get out of the limo and walk them around to El Diablo. Once the girls had been handed off to El Diablo, the man retreated back into the darkened interior. Winter had looked back over her shoulder, her gaze clinging to his departing frame. The man had made eye contact with her once before nodding his head encouragingly at her. Winter had hardened her features and put her head up proudly in response.

Darcy just knew she was going to throw up. This was a day of mixed emotions. On the one hand, she was finally going to see fucking Rayburn get what he so justly deserved. She hoped Cain made him suffer. On the other, she wasn't sure how much she could watch. Not only that, but she had to confront him herself. She'd demanded that privilege. If she had to relive it, he would too. So would her mother. Even though she dreaded all of that, her worst fear, the thing that made her wake up at night sweating and clinging to Viper, was the possibility that he'd never look at her the same after this. She had truly been a victim. True, she'd taken her destiny into her own hands later, but for that one brief moment, she'd been a terrified little girl, powerless to do anything other than allow the abuse.

A second car pulled into the drive. This time, a screeching Donna was hauled out, her arms tied behind her while Rayburn was pulled from the trunk and dumped unceremoniously onto the ground in the wet snow. Neither looked to be any worse for wear. No obvious bruising or like they'd been mistreated in any way. Pity. After everything, Darcy wanted to see them suffer. It was petty of her, she knew, but if anyone deserved it, they did.

El Diablo approached Cain. The expression on his face was one of grave reverence. He stuck out his hand. Cain took it immediately. The two men met gazes, and something seemed to pass between them. Darcy had learned to admire Cain and the way he interacted with everyone in the club. Everyone deferred to him, but not in a subservient way. It was as if he'd earned the right to be their president and he took the responsibility seriously.

"As requested," El Diablo said. "Your intel man should have the files I sent you on the couple as well as the girls."

"We do," Cain said.

Data cleared his throat and raised a finger to get the men's attention. "I have one question. It doesn't pertain to the information so much as how you obtained it."

The corner of El Diablo's lips twitched. "Ask your question, brother."

Data gritted his teeth, not used to anyone other than those in Bones referring to him as a brother. "How did you know who we were looking for?"

"I'm rather embarrassed to admit how," El Diablo admitted. "I understand you have a contact on the dark web you work with occasionally."

"You'll not convince me Panther ratted me out. We've worked together too long."

"He didn't rat you out so much as bring to my attention we could help Bones."

Data groaned, cursing under his breath. "I knew better," he muttered. "Fucking *knew* better."

"Relax, brother. He had no intention of undercutting you. He merely wanted to help. He knew I wanted to convince young Magenta to talk with me and thought it might go a long way toward bridging the gap between us."

"What is Panther to you?"

"He's is my protégé. Son of a rival who sold him to me when he was a young boy as payment for one of his many sins. I raised him as my own. So, in essence, he wanted the meeting with Magenta as much as I did." He turned to Magenta then. "Forgive me, my dear, but there is nothing I won't do to get into your good graces. I truly only want a relationship with you. A chance, as it were, to be the father I never had the chance to be."

Magenta gripped Sword's hand, still uncomfortable, but clearly wanting to believe El Diablo. "She'll consider it carefully," Sword answered for her. "We both will."

"That's all I could ask for." El Diablo made a sweeping gesture toward the two adults, hands zip-tied behind their backs. "I present Rayburn and Donna Mills. In exchange for permission to give my daughter a permanent way to contact me at her leisure, I'll wait here to… assume responsibility for the couple after you've judged them."

That was a new development. Cain raised his eyebrows. "You'll dispose of the two if we kill them. You'll give us your personal guarantee no one will ever find the bodies or be able to trace the disappearances back to Bones?"

"Guaranteed. My word as El Diablo."

Cain looked to Viper. His woman's tormenters, his call.

"The offer is much appreciated," Viper said, "but we clean up our own messes. To ask another club to take on that challenge is too much even for a sister club."

Cain gave a sharp nod, approving of his decision. "No offense intended. Anything done permanently to another isn't taken lightly by Bones. If we feel the couple needs to die, we'll be the one to take care of the deed in its entirety."

Donna whimpered while Rayburn blustered. "You can't do this! The state police will be all over this place! We'll be missed! I'm an important businessman!"

"You're an important businessman who embezzled from your company and lost it all gambling," El Diablo said, waving a negligent hand. "True, your company will be looking for you, but they will lose your trail after your plane leaves for Vegas with a one-way ticket to Moscow."

Rayburn's jaw slackened. "I didn't book a flight to Moscow! I hadn't won enough money yet!"

"Oh, but you did book the flight. Your passport was used for you to board the plane. It left about eleven hours ago, I believe. And the hotel books show you did, indeed, win a substantial amount of money before making your purchase. Oh, and one more thing." El Diablo got right up in Rayburn's face. "The men you had planned on selling your daughters to were *my* men. On your tail. Tracking you down to return you to your judgment day."

"How did they know we were planning on going to Moscow?" Donna demanded. "You said no one knew! You said we could disappear and live a life of luxury!"

"I don't know how they knew!" Rayburn snapped. "But I hadn't made any arrangements. Anyone following the trail will figure that out. Who skips the country to Moscow, of all places, without a plan?" The look of triumph on his face made Darcy want to claw his fucking eyes out.

"I'm afraid you did," El Diablo said. "At least, that's what we've made it look like. Lucky for you, Moscow doesn't have an extradition treaty with the U.S., so you can live out your life there. Well." He grinned. "That's what it will look like to anyone looking into your disappearance." He smirked evilly. "On the other hand, if you stay in the U.S., you'll be arrested for a myriad of charges, including child pornography and sex trafficking. The proof is ready to be sent discreetly to the FBI should anything go unexpectedly here today. By unexpectedly, I mean that you live to walk out of here. No matter what happens to you now, Rayburn, your life as you knew it is over."

For the first time, Darcy started to feel a sense of power. These men were systematically tearing Rayburn's life apart. Just as he'd done to her.

"We should go inside," Cain said. "Basement, if you please, Bohannon." The enforcer and Torpedo escorted the couple to the basement. In one section of the vast space, there was a meeting table for all the officers of Bones, as well as places for spectators in the club. In front of the table, the accused would be shackled to a chair bolted to the floor. They would be interrogated and judgment would be passed. After that, well, it would depend on the degree of guilt. Darcy honestly wasn't certain what she hoped for. She didn't want these men to have to kill the two people who had made her life a living hell. She was fine now. She had a man who loved and protected her and would be there for her. He hadn't said as much, but she felt it in the way he touched her. The way he made love to her.

Once everyone was settled, El Diablo and Black Reign outside with a select group of prospects and patched members, Cain rapped on the table twice in quick succession, a sign for everyone to settle down.

"You can't do this," Donna all but sobbed. "We have rights!"

"If you can't be silent, we'll gag you until it's time for you to give your account," Cain said off-handedly. When neither Donna nor Rayburn spoke, he began the proceedings.

"We have been provided with a file from one of Data's contacts regarding crimes against you," Cain began, "rangin' from rape to human trafficking, to theft. I'm leavin' off the theft accusations as I don't really give a rat's ass about shit like that. I am concerned with the other two. Specifically how it pertains to your three daughters."

Darcy noticed that Winter and Serelda were in the corner of the room. They clung to each other, sitting in a chair huddled together. Winter put herself in front of her sister. Darcy had never given thought to the sisters' individual personalities. Mostly, she'd avoided them as well as their father as much as she could. Now, she was ashamed she hadn't reached out to the two women. They might have been older than her, but she was obviously the strongest of the three.

"Your daughters have been through enough, from what I've gathered. We took their statements from the report given to us by Data's source, who just happens to be the protégé of El Diablo. She had no reason to manufacture information, and we're taking everything she said as the facts as best she was able to gather. She drew no supposition, but stuck with information she was able to gather, itemizing everything carefully. All of it from the past week and a half. As such, we have no reason to believe their ordeal hadn't been going on for some time."

"That's not fair!" Rayburn exploded, his face red in his anger. "I want my lawyer! He'll put a stop to this farce! I've got my rights! This isn't even a fucking court! Who the hell do you people think you are?"

Cain leaned forward. "Do I look like I give a damn about your rights? For that matter, do I look like the kind of man who gives a fuck about whether or not you have your lawyer? We don't muddle the facts with legal mumbo jumbo." He leaned back, his hand on the table. "You'll have your chance to answer for yourself."

Rayburn lifted his chin. "I did nothing but try to be the best parent I could."

"I see," Cain said. He looked to Viper and nodded. Darcy knew this was it. Her heart pounded and her palms were sweaty. She gripped Viper's hand tightly, not wanting to let go. Just looking at Rayburn made her skin crawl.

"If you don't want to do this, you can always tell me and Cain in private. Or Angel and Magenta."

"No." She swallowed. "I need to do this. No matter how embarrassing or humiliating."

She felt him growl where her shoulder rested against his chest. The man was the most protective, wonderful man she'd ever met in her life. It was his protectiveness alone that gave her the courage to do this.

She raised her chin, still clinging to Viper, needing him to know she still needed him even after this was over. "What do you want to know?"

Cain looked her straight in the eye, neither encouraging nor intimidating her. He was, for all intents and purposes, impassive as any judge. This was about the finding the truth before passing judgment.

"You know that bitch will say anything to make me look bad," Rayburn grumbled. "She's just jealous of mine and my daughters' place in Donna's life. Always was from the moment she met us."

"Gag him," Cain said mildly. Darcy could see Viper took great pleasure in watching as Bohannon stuffed a rag in the man's mouth and secured it with duct tape. He smirked at the other man, gripping Darcy's hand a little tighter. Rayburn glared daggers at her, and it was all she could do not to shrink into Viper for comfort. He seemed to realize this and put his arm around her protectively.

"I want to know," Cain said, drawing her attention back to him, "why you felt the need to run into the wilderness in the middle of a snowstorm. Then, instead of welcoming help to get back to civilization, you fought, going to far as to tell Viper and Arkham you'd never go back to that molesting bastard."

She took a deep breath. This was it. Viper would know she was a coward. Would know she'd been touched by someone as vile as Rayburn Mills and hadn't fought back. "The night I ran, Rayburn attacked me." Mills mumbled angrily, fighting his bonds, but unable to say anything because of the gag. "But he'd been leading up to it for a long time. I'd wake up in the middle of the night with him standing over me, masturbating." She shuddered and even stumbled over the word. "He's disgusting," she said under her breath. She looked at Viper, willing him to understand she hated every second. He nodded at her, telling her to go on. "No matter how I barricaded my door, he always managed to get in. I'd wake up and there he'd be. Standing over me. He'd just smirk. Like he'd beaten me by making it into my bedroom without me waking up. Anyway, the night I took off, he must have been standing there longer than usual because he was not only yanking his prick, he was on the verge of getting off." She shuddered, unable to hide her disgust. "I heard him groaning, and opened my eyes, prepared to move away from him and scream until he left, but the second I looked at him, he came. Like all over me. Bastard wasn't quiet about it either. I was so startled, I couldn't move. The next thing I knew, he was on top of me."

Viper growled, his fists clenching. Darcy had to look away from him, unable to see the disgust she knew would be on his face. Nothing she'd ever done or been through compared to the humiliation in admitting what her stepfather had done to her. It was bad enough she had to recount it in front of her newfound father and people she was becoming to think of as friends, but Viper was there to witness it all. How would she ever face him again?

"Did he rape you, Darcy?" Cain asked gently. There was compassion in his voice, but it bordered too close to pity for Darcy. She stuck her chin up. Now if she could ignore the tears tracking down her cheeks, she might not feel so humiliated. "No. He tried, but I got my wits about me enough to fight him off. My alarm clock was on the nightstand, and I clocked him with it." She hoped her pun would ease the tension, but it was a pitiful attempt at best. "I hit him until he didn't move. Then I crawled out from under him, packed my backpack, and got the fuck outta there." She shrugged, trying to pretend like it was all no big deal. "Five days later, Bones found me."

"Was that the first time he'd actually touched you?" Cain asked his question calmly, but there was an underlying current of anger. Perhaps he was angry at her for dragging them into something like this when the man hadn't actually sexually assaulted her. I mean, she'd gotten spooged on. Big deal. A little bukkake never hurt anyone, right?

"The first time he had the nerve to try."

Cain nodded, staring down Rayburn. Then he turned his attention to Donna. "What about your mother?"

"What about her? And don't call her my mother. She might have given birth to me, but she was never a mother."

"I see." He thumbed through the papers in his hand, the muscle in his jaw ticking like a son of a bitch. She was too afraid to look at Viper. "She know about any of this?"

"She knew enough. Told me once it didn't matter how young I was, he'd get tired of me and come running back to her. That was the night before I left."

"Did you know of either of them mistreating your stepsisters?"

There it was. The real shame. She supposed it was better to get it all out now than to have to keep suffering one defeat after another.

"I didn't." She wanted to leave it at that, but knew she couldn't. "But then, I never looked into it. I never thought they might be in the same boat as me." She gave a long, shuddering sigh. "Looking back, I suppose I should have."

"No one is blaming you for anything, Darcy," Viper said quietly.

"Well, maybe they should," she snapped. Turning to her stepsisters she met their gazes boldly. "I was wrong to not get close to you guys. I was just ducking my head and staying out of the way. I should have stopped to consider you might need my help as much as I could have used yours."

"You had no idea," Winter said softly. "We knew to pretend everything was fine. It kept anyone from looking too closely at us."

"The last thing we needed was for Dad to find out we had a friend willing to help us," Serelda added, her voice a bare thread of sound. "The one time we thought we were free, he let us try, then laughed when he pulled us back into the very net we tried to escape."

"The men he gave us to that night were brutal." Winter stood, walking slowly, as if in a trance, toward Rayburn. "Weren't they, Daddy?" She asked the question like an innocent little girl asking a simple question of her father. The look of hatred on her face told another story altogether. As she crossed in front of the couple, she slowly, deliberately pulled a wicked-looking knife from her boot. "They played with us all night while you kept an eye on us, didn't they? 'They just want to play, sweetheart,'" she said in a mocking tone, obviously a repeat of what Rayburn had told his daughters on the night in question. "'Play nice, girls,'" she said.

The whole scene was eerie as fuck. Like something out of a horror film. Winter was on the offensive while Serelda was still curled in a ball on the couch, watching everything in silence.

Winter struck out with the knife, slicing a thin cut down Rayburn's neck. Nothing too deep. Just enough for it to leak a thin trickle of blood down his skin to his shirt. Rayburn howled, his eyes wide, but unable to get free or speak because of his bonds and gag.

"They sliced at us," Winter continued. "Made us bleed until it felt like our whole bodies were slick with it." She made another cut on her father, this time deeper and on his shoulder. "You know what? I wanna watch you bleed now. *Daddy*."

This time, Winter stabbed the knife in the side of Rayburn's neck sideways, clean to the hilt. The she pulled it out and did it again. And again.

And again.

Blood arched across the room to the sounds of Donna's screams. The coppery scent was nearly overwhelming. Darcy wanted to gag. At the same time, she wanted to pick up a knife and help Winter. But Rayburn wasn't hers to kill. He was all Winter's. All the while, Serelda never made a sound. Just watched on in silence, a little satisfied smile on her face.

Finally, an arm snaked around Winter's waist, pulling her away but in no way restraining her. It was the man from El Diablo's limo. He murmured to her, soothing a wild animal. Winter threw the knife down at the body of her father and spat before going to her sister, urging the other woman to her feet and going with the man from Black Reign.

"Don't take kindly to another club entering our meetings," Cain said as the other man led the women to the stairs.

He turned, nodding at Cain. "The girls needed to know someone had their backs. I apologize for invading your territory."

"I assume you're taking them with you?" Cain referred to Winter and Serelda. Darcy wanted to protest. She wanted the chance to get to know her stepsisters. Viper put a hand on her shoulder, preventing her from going to the two women.

"I am."

"They want to go?"

Winter turned to Cain, blood covering her from the arterial spray she'd just unleashed. She looked like an innocent child, her expression nearly dead. "No one will ever make me do anything I don't want to ever again," she said evenly. No inflection. "I'm going with El Segador. Serelda wants to go, too." Apparently, the man traveling with El Diablo was, quite literally, the Reaper.

Confirming her sister's statement, Serelda stood and threaded her fingers through Winter's. The three of them left the room, leaving a trail of blood in their wake.

Chapter Nine

Viper could see Darcy was hurting. The whole thing had taken something from her he wasn't certain she had to give. The one thing he hated about meetings like this was the formality of them. Cain allowed any of the officers to have free say and the patched members to question with permission, but he wasn't the same man Darcy was accustomed to. Neither was he. During times like this, every man in Bones had to be as dispassionate as they could be. Otherwise, killings happened when they might not be deserved. Other times, it allowed nature to take its course. Like tonight.

Rayburn Mills had it coming. It was only fitting the ones he'd caused the most pain had been the ones to do him in. Now, it was the woman's turn. Donna Mills.

"Darcy," Cain said softly. "With everything we've heard from you, and the report we have, there's no question Donna is guilty." Cain purposefully didn't refer to Donna Mills as Darcy's mother. "As the ones Rayburn tormented most passed sentence on him, you have the opportunity to do so with Donna."

The woman turned pleading eyes to Darcy, darting her gaze to the body of her dead husband lying in a pool of his own blood beside her. "You can't possibly, Darcy. I'm your mother!"

"I never remember you being a mother to me." Darcy's voice was quiet, resigned. "You deserve everything Rayburn got and more. You may not have done the deed yourself, but you knew what he was doing."

"I didn't know. Not until that night. I swear."

"Really? They why did you lash out at *me* instead of him? I'm your flesh and blood! Me!" Darcy had worked herself up now. Getting angry. Viper thought it was a good thing. She needed to let out her anger. There was no way he was going to allow her to kill her mother, but Donna didn't need to know that. Neither did Darcy. "Instead of finding out exactly what he'd been doing or, heaven forbid, turning your anger toward him, you turned on me. Accused me of trying to sleep with him! Do you have any idea how disgusting that is?"

"I didn't mean it, Darcy, baby. I swear! I was just hurt."

"Ever think I might have been hurting, too?" Darcy let out a puff of air. All the fight seemed to go out of her. "But it wasn't me you hurt the most. It was Winter and Serelda."

"I didn't do anything to them. I swear."

"You swear a lot, don't you? Too bad no one believes it when you do. You knew Rayburn had planned on going to Moscow, so you knew he'd need a lot of money. Tell me why I shouldn't believe you didn't know he'd planned on selling Winter and Serelda into sexual slavery?"

Donna just looked at her, either unwilling to admit she knew or unable to deny she did. It was pointless and they all knew it. "So that's it then." Donna scoffed. "You're just like him." She jerked her chin at Data. "He's as much a killer as the rest of them. And you're no better."

"They didn't kill Rayburn, Donna. His demons finally caught up with him. If Winter wanted him dead, she'd earned the right to do it herself. But you?" Darcy shook her head. "If anyone earned the right to kill you it was Winter or Serelda. They were the ones who suffered most. I fought back the only way I knew how. I always hated Calvin for sending me off to summer camps all the time, but I suppose I need to look him up and thank him. If it hadn't been for him, I'd have been just as bad off as my sisters." She looked to Data. "Donna took your family away from you. With Winter and Serelda gone, I think it only fitting you be the one to decide her fate. I'm done with her."

Darcy turned her back on her mother and ducked her head, but not before Viper saw the sheen of tears. He took the three steps separating them and snagged her chin in his big hand, forcing her to look up at him.

"Stay with me, Lil' Bit. Focus on me."

She took a breath and nodded shakily, pursing her lips together tightly. Viper desperately wanted to pull her into his arms and take her away from all this, but he couldn't. Not because Cain would stop him. Because Darcy would never forgive him. She needed him there, might even need him to physically remove her from the situation, but she'd never see it that way. She'd stood up and given voice to something that was obviously deeply humiliating and terrifying. She had to see the rest through to the bitter end.

Cain raised an eyebrow at Data. He shook his head. "I have my daughter now. She's safe, if a bit worse for wear. If she refuses to pass judgment on Donna, then I won't either." He nodded to his president. "I'm not sure where that leaves us."

"As it happens," El Diablo said from the corner of the room near the stairs. Apparently, as El Segador had exited, El Diablo had taken his place. "I may have a solution."

"Of course you do," Cain muttered. "When this is over, I'm havin' me a talk with some fuckin' prospects and a few patched members to boot. What the fuck are you doin' down here? This is a closed meeting."

"For this very purpose," he answered, his signature dashing smile firmly in place. "Little Donna here went along with a horrendous future for her stepdaughters. She might not have orchestrated it, but she didn't try to stop it. In fact, she stood to profit from it as much as Rayburn did."

"Your point, El Diablo?"

"Give her to me. I know of some men deprived of the company of her stepdaughters who might be willing to take her instead."

Donna paled. "You can't possibly."

"Oh, I assure you he can," Cain said, standing. "And it sounds like the perfect punishment. An eye for an eye, as it were." He nodded at El Diablo, who spoke into a mic at his wrist, calling for his men.

Donna screamed and begged until they gagged her, tying her legs and feet together and putting a bag over her head. A big man pulled her to her feet, then hefted her over his shoulder to carry her out.

Viper could see Darcy's distress. "If you want to stop this, now's the time. Once they leave, it's done."

"No," she said. "I hate it, but she made her own bed. What she and Rayburn did was inexcusable. I doubt they'd have gotten justice if they'd gone through the normal system so this is the best way."

Viper nodded, scooping her up into his arms. "We're done," he told Cain. "I'll see you later for the debriefing."

"No rush. See to your woman."

Darcy put her arms around his neck and buried her face there as he took them through the common room. Suzie saw them and ran straight to Viper.

"Is Darcy OK?"

"She's fine," Viper said, not slowing until Darcy raised her head, wiping her face with one hand.

"Let me down, Viper." She was quiet, but sounded more in control than she looked. He stopped, setting her gently on her feet.

Darcy opened her arms to little Suzie. The girl had tears in her eyes. "I was afraid," she said. "The others left and Stunner wouldn't let me watch. I was afraid you'd left, too."

"I'm not going anywhere," she said, pulling Suzie into her arms for a fierce hug. "This is my home now."

With a glad cry, Suzie tightened her thin arms around Darcy's neck. "I'm so glad! You're the best friend I ever had!" When Stunner grunted, giving the child a brows-drawn look of hurt, she giggled. "My *second* best friend, then." She turned to Stunner. "I still love you best."

Viper put his hand on Darcy's shoulder. He wanted to allow her time with the girl, but he knew Darcy was still fragile. She needed some time to herself. Some time to come to terms with everything that had happened over the past few weeks. "Let's go, Lil' Bit. I'll bring her down first thing in the morning, Suzie. Right now, she needs rest."

Viper took her straight to his room, intending to run her a hot bath and spend an hour massaging her shoulders while she decompressed. Once inside with the door shut, however, Darcy took his mouth with a white-hot heat that seared away any good intentions he might have had. There was no denying her when she wanted to lose herself in his body. He was fine with it and was pleased that she looked to him when she needed something.

She kissed him with her whole heart. No woman could not love a man and kiss him the way she was kissing him now. Every flick of her tongue brought him back to her when he knew he could have happily left her in Data's care to deliver her mother to the doom she'd brought down on herself.

No. Darcy needed him here. Needed him to drive the memory of what she'd just witnessed out of her mind with his body. His love.

His love!

Sweet God above, he truly did love her. With everything inside him. He would have gladly suffered a thousand deaths to take the pain in her life away. He wished he could have made it so she'd had her father's protection. Had Data known about her, been a part of her life, she might have had a very different life thus far. And a different future, possibly not with him. As much as he wanted and needed her, as much as he knew he'd do anything he had to in order to keep her with him, Viper knew he'd have given everything for the opportunity and privilege to spare her the pain she'd gone through.

"I need you," she whimpered, pulling off his shirt to scratch her nails down his chest. Viper threw his head back, savoring the moment, the sweet pain of it.

"You have me, Lil' Bit." He pulled at her clothing, needing her naked because that was what she needed. "And I'm going to worship every inch of your body."

Darcy made a little sound of need, her fingers wrapping around his cock before he could get his pants off completely. She sank to her knees and swallowed him down in a long, wet, greedy gulp.

Viper's knees threatened to buckle as she gripped the fronts of his thighs.

Her mouth worked him like nothing he'd ever experienced. Her fingers dug into his skin deep around the bunching muscles of his legs. Then she slid one hand around and gripped his buttocks, gripping and squeezing in time with the sucking movement of her mouth. She didn't let up, sucking him like she intended to make him come before she let up. Which wasn't happening.

OK, it might be happening.

She looked up at him with those stunning pale blue eyes and Viper had to bite the inside of his cheek to keep himself under control. Every muscle in his body tensed as he fought off the inevitable. Darcy had one goal in mind, and that was making him lose his Goddamned mind.

She pumped him with one hand while urging him on with the other gripping his ass. Taking him as deep as she could. Viper actually felt the back of her throat. She didn't pull back either. Just kept looking up at him with those gorgeous eyes of hers.

"Let me go, baby," he managed to croak out. "Let me go before I blow my load."

She just opened those eyes wider, gripping his ass tighter, taking him deeper. God almighty! How was a man supposed to fight this? How was he supposed to push her away from him when she obviously wanted this as much as he did?

"Woman…" He gave her one last warning.

Darcy let go of his ass and he thought she was giving him a reprieve. Instead, she dipped her hand between her legs, then raised her hand up, offering her own moisture to him. To suck while he came.

With a vicious snarl, Viper snagged her wrist in one hand and tunneled his fingers into her silky hair, fucking her mouth while he tasted her. Before the night was out, he intended to replay this, only with his mouth between her legs. Because he was definitely coming right where he stood.

His cock swelled between her lush lips, his balls tightening. Darcy continued to look up at him, holding him captive with her gaze and the suction of her mouth on his aching cock.

"Can't hold back," he bit out. "Can't stop! AHHHH!" Head thrown back, Viper roared to the ceiling. His seed exploded from him with such force, he was afraid she couldn't take him. The sudden image of the ugliness she'd described earlier flashed into his mind, and he knew he never wanted to see her like that, even if it was him she was covered in. He would not do that to her, never wanted her to associate anything they did with her past. It was enough for him to regain control even in the midst of the intense pleasure she'd created in him.

When he felt the force lessen, Viper pulled himself free of that hot, wet haven, needing to contain anything she couldn't swallow. A few ribbons of seed dribbled down his length, but Darcy refused to give him up. She leaned in and took him in her mouth again, lapping up every drop he had to give, squeezing the head so that she milked the last of him free.

"I don't want to make a mess on you," he murmured. "Let me clean up."

"*I'm* cleaning you, Viper. I want this from you, and you're going to give it to me."

He barked out a laugh. Yes. He was. Anything his girl wanted, she would have. "I want you in the bed," he finally managed to get out. "Want to suck that pretty little pussy until you come just as hard as I did."

"Yes," she breathed. "I want that, too." Darcy reluctantly let go of his cock, and he pulled her to her feet. Scooping her up into his arms, Viper took her to bed, laying her down gently before crawling between her legs. He parted her slick folds with his big fingers and just gazed at her for several moments. She was exquisite. So fucking beautiful his heart hurt.

As he lowered his head and swiped at her with his tongue, he murmured, "Never get enough of the taste of you." His voice was husky, needy with lust. "Want this every fuckin' night for the rest of my Goddamned life!"

Her pussy was sweet heaven. Nothing could ever compare with her taste, the way she gripped him when he fucked her. Nothing. Her clit throbbed under his tongue. When he slid two fingers inside her, she cried out, thrusting her hips at him, begging for more. Viper gladly obliged.

Looking at her as she thrashed under him, thrusting her hips at him, Viper knew he'd never before seen a woman to compare to her. She was giving him everything she had, her whole self. His woman. Darcy. So Goddamned beautiful it nearly hurt to look at her. How anyone in the world could want to hurt her was beyond any reason. Right there, Viper vowed no one ever would again. He'd protect her with his fucking life.

Viper didn't let up until she came in a wet rush around his fingers, her cunt pulsing and milking him like she would his cock. He growled and snarled, lapping up all she had to give him and pushing her for more.

"Mmmm." The sound was rough and gravelly, more an animalistic growl than masculine appreciation. "I think your little pussy wants filled with my cum. Look how it's milking my fingers."

"Oh, God! Viper! Yes! Do that! I want it!" Darcy looked up at him, her gaze big and round. Her eyes were glassy with lust and need, beyond reason.

"I'm clean, baby. You know I'd never do anything to harm you. Right?"

Her brow furrowed as she was obviously trying to understand his train of thought. "I -- oh! I am, too." She reached for him, clutching at him until he covered her with his large frame. "I need you inside me, Viper." Her little whimper was all the encouragement he needed.

"You have me, Lil' Bit," he said before tucking the head of his cock against her pussy and surging home in one hard, sure thrust.

Darcy cried out, wrapping her lithe legs around him to lock at the small of his back. She used that leverage to match him thrust for thrust, doing her best to urge him to move faster and faster. Sweat erupted over her skin, making them glide against each other like silk over satin.

More than anything Viper wanted to fuck her like this forever, to keep her on the thin razor's edge without letting her tip over into an orgasm. Realistically, he knew it was impossible, but he kept her there as long as he could. Several times, she bit him, snarling her frustration. He refused to give in to her. She threatened to unman him, but he just bit her back and growled while he fucked her, always shifting his body away from her clit as best he could to prolong the agony.

And it was agony. A desperate attempt to both reach and stave off the ultimate pleasure like he'd never done before. Darcy was a mindless thing, writhing in his arms, her body shuddering with pleasure without ever reaching her climax. It wasn't until tears streaked down her temples that Viper took pity on her. She was ready.

Shifting his position just that little bit, Viper wrapped his arms tightly around her and growled one command into her ear. "Come!"

She did.

Her whole body tensing, Darcy screamed to the ceiling, a shrill, echoing shriek that told Viper she was obeying him. Her cunt spasmed around him, pulsing with every wave of pleasure that ruled her body. She alternately went limp then clung to him, her body worn out and unsure what it needed. Darcy looked glassy-eyed, like she was dazed and confused as to what had just happened to her, but her gaze clung to him as much as her body did.

When she was finally still, Viper surged into her freely until he reached his own orgasm. He bared his teeth and roared as he pumped more and more cum into her. He wanted to mark her in the only way he could. Fill her with seed. Drain himself in her.

It took long, long moments for his cock to subside. When it did, Viper thought he might die, he was so weak. He collapsed onto Darcy, his lips at her neck over her rapidly beating pulse. She still clung to him with arms and legs, her fingers tunneling in the hair at the nape of his neck and stroking a soothing rhythm. He couldn't catch his breath, and she seemed to be breathing just as hard.

"You OK? I didn't hurt you, did I?"

"Never," she gasped out. "It was so wonderful."

Viper lifted his head to find her lips with his, kissing her gently. The stirring of her tongue against his brought his cock back to life when he knew he had no hope of sating himself again. Not right now. Still, he swelled inside her. Her pussy gave a little squeeze around him and he chuckled.

"My greedy little girl. Are you wanting my cock again already?"

She shrugged, giving him a saucy grin. "Maybe. You got hard quick enough. I think you're as greedy for me as I am for you."

"Damned straight," he answered, still kissing her with lazy flicks of his tongue. He couldn't help but thrust into her again. Just the feel of her around him was enough to make him need her. "You may end up killing me, you know that?"

"Death by sex?"

He chuckled. "Yeah. Something like that. But hey, I'll die with a smile on my face."

"Or my cunt on your face." She bit his bottom lip sharply. Viper laughed, never stopping the lazy circles of his hips as he continued to fuck her. The mixture of both their cum coated his balls and inner thighs, a sensation Viper found highly stimulating under the circumstances. It was enough to make his cock pulse once again, eager for another go.

"Or your cunt on my face," he agreed. "Either way would be acceptable."

"How about we forgo the dying part and just get you to come inside me again," she whispered, a wicked temptress in his ear. "You're so hot inside me, Viper. I want to feel it again."

"Fuck," he swore before kissing her again. This time, he thrust his tongue deep. Just like his cock thrust deep inside her pussy.

"I love fuckin' you, Darcy," he admitted. "If I live to be a hundred, I'll be fuckin' you every Goddamned day."

"I love fucking you, too. Especially with your big body pinning me down like this. I'm helpless underneath you."

He couldn't help but growl, the ache in his cock building with a vengeance. "Gonna fill you again, woman," he bit out. "But you gotta take it if you want it. You gotta come for me again. Squeeze my cock with that little cunt."

She cried out sharply, but shook her head as if trying to fight off the rising pleasure. "Viper!" Her hands gripped his ass, urging him forward, but he meant what he'd said. He snagged her wrists and pinned them above her head, continuing to fuck her, but with more vigor now. There was no way to stop it. The aggression built in him when she tried to resist him and his body needed to dominate hers.

"You do as I tell you," he growled, nipping the side of her neck again. His hips snapped forward and back, fucking her harder with each stroke. "I want you to come for me. On me. Milk me so I fill you with cum, woman!"

Her breathing became erratic, her face and neck flushing as the orgasm finally overtook her. Darcy gave another shrill scream as her body finally gave in to the orgasm she fought. When her cunt clamped down on him, Viper let her take him with her into bliss. The pleasure was raw, uncivilized, and violent in its intensity. Stars floated at the edges of his vision and he fought not to pass out. The sheer force of his ejaculation took him by surprise and he cried out with her, unable to do anything other than follow where she took him. He might have ruled her body with his superior strength, but Darcy was the one who'd dominated him. It felt right. He'd given her what she wanted, had helped her forget the ugliness of what had happened if only for a few minutes, but he was confident enough in his ability to read her that he knew he'd consumed her.

"Viper," she sighed, her face aglow with pleasure, her lips curled in a genuine smile. "I... I love you so much!"

"Ah, baby," he said, letting her arms go as he rolled them to their side. He kissed her gently before cupping her face in one of his big hands. "I love you, too. I'm yours as long as you'll have me."

"I'm yours too."

He hugged her for long minutes, never separating their bodies. He was sated for the moment, mainly because he knew she was sated, but his cock was still semi-hard as if to tell her he could give her all the pleasure she wanted whenever she wanted it.

Viper cleared his throat. "I want you to wear my property patch," he said, gruffly. "I'll get your vest as soon as I can have it made."

She smiled, but looked up at him in confusion. "OK."

"That means I want you to be my ol' lady. For me, it's the same as being married." She opened her mouth, but he pressed on. "I know you'll want a ring and a ceremony and all that shit, and I can give you that. But once I tell everyone you're my property and you wear my patch, it's done. You got that?" He sounded a bit bossier than he intended, but really. He wasn't asking her. If he ordered her to do it, she couldn't actually reject him. Right?

Darcy giggled. "You're such a dork." When he growled at her, she leaned in and nipped his chin.

"Don't think I don't know what you're doing. I'd still say no if I didn't want you." She grinned. "But I do want you, so I'll accept anything you want me to do. Just make sure you fuck me good every chance you get, and we'll be good."

Viper couldn't help himself. He laughed heartily, wrapping his arms around her tightly. "I hear you, baby."

They lay like that for a long time. Viper dozed lightly, his hand lazily petting her ass just because he could.

"Viper?"

"Um?"

"Do you think El Diablo will kill Donna?"

Fuck. He sighed. "I don't know, Lil' Bit. I won't lie to you. Ever. So, if he does, it won't be outright. She was as much a part of whatever happened to your stepsisters as Mills was. I got the feeling that her punishment had more to do with them than it did you."

"Yeah. Me too. That's why I didn't protest. They were hurt much more than I was. I just hope they forgive me. I never would have left them alone if I'd thought they were in trouble."

"I think they know that. Given the situation, you couldn't be expected to bond with them. Mills made sure of that. He was smart enough to know Serelda and Winter wouldn't reach out to you. By making you the outsider, he guaranteed you wouldn't reach out to them either."

"Maybe." She sighed. "I think, at some point, I need to try to get to know them. Maybe we could help each other heal?"

"I think that's the best idea," Viper said, stroking her back gently before letting his hand rest on her ass once again.

Again, they fell into a peaceful silence. Viper continued to pet her, hoping to soothe her. His cock had gone soft and slipped from her body, a fact he lamented greatly.

"You know, Christmas is in a couple of weeks," she said. "Maybe we could plan something for Christmas morning?"

It took Viper a moment to realize what she meant, then he grinned. "You mean, a Christmas wedding?"

"Yeah."

"I think we could do that. I'm sure the girls would be thrilled to help you put it together."

"I'd really like that, Viper."

"Then you'll have it, Lil' Bit." He turned her in his arms to kiss her tenderly. "You'll have it. Merry Christmas, baby."

"Yeah," she answered with a sigh. "Merry Christmas."

Marteeka Karland

Erotic romance author by night, emergency room tech/clerk by day, Marteeka Karland works really hard to drive everyone in her life completely and totally nuts. She has been creating stories from her warped imagination since she was in the third grade. Her love of writing blossomed throughout her teenage years until it developed into the totally unorthodox and irreverent style her English teachers tried so hard to rid her of.

Marteeka at Changeling: changelingpress.com/marteeka-karland-a-39

Changeling Press E-Books

More Sci-Fi, Fantasy, Paranormal, and BDSM adventures available in e-book format for immediate download at ChangelingPress.com -- Werewolves, Vampires, Dragons, Shapeshifters and more -- Erotic Tales from the edge of your imagination.

What are E-Books?

E-books, or electronic books, are books designed to be read in digital format -- on your desktop or laptop computer, notebook, tablet, Smart Phone, or any electronic e-book reader.

Where can I get Changeling Press E-Books?

Changeling Press e-books are available at ChangelingPress.com, Amazon, Apple Books, Barnes & Noble, and Kobo/Walmart.

ChangelingPress.com

Made in the USA
Columbia, SC
17 December 2024

49708454R00122